DREAD WOOD
FEAR GROUND

For the Reid family, with love.

First published in Great Britain in 2022 by Farshore
An imprint of HarperCollins*Publishers*
1 London Bridge Street, London SE1 9GF

farshore.co.uk

HarperCollins*Publishers*
1st Floor, Watermarque Building, Ringsend Road
Dublin 4, Ireland

Text copyright © Jennifer Killick 2022
Illustration copyright © Tom Clohosy Cole 2022

The moral rights of the author and illustrator have been asserted

ISBN 978 0 7555 0462 6

Printed and bound in the UK using 100% renewable electricity at
CPI Group (UK) Ltd

1

A CIP catalogue record for this title is available from the British Library.

JENNIFER KILLICK

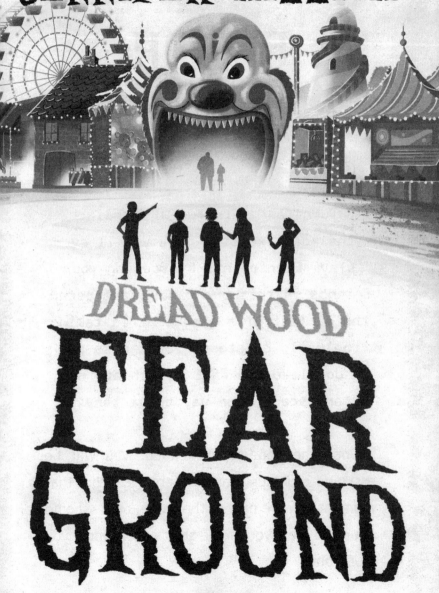

DREAD WOOD

FEAR GROUND

Farshore

FLINCH:
A PLAYER'S GUIDE

Turn fear into fun with 'Flinch'
–the most exciting game you'll ever
play. Earn points by scaring your
friends in this brand new, fast-paced,
thrill-fest of a game that is taking
the world by storm. Don't miss out
– download the FREE Flinch app now
and scare your way to victory.

Once the app is downloaded, you will be
assigned a unique player reference. From that
moment you are part of the game, and – should
your app alert you of the start of a round – you
MUST play.

The Flinch app selects players using geographical location, so being in an area where a large number of players are collected increases the chances of a round being announced.

The players selected will be notified of the start of a round by the Flinch tune playing on their mobile devices. The Flinch tune is 'Pop Goes the Weasel', a nursery rhyme used in traditional jack-in-the-box toys. Imagine turning the handle on the box, winding it slowly towards a jump-scare. Players have until the music stops to take their places, ready to play.

When the first part of the Flinch tune stops playing, there will be an undetermined number of minutes for gameplay, during which players must try to score as many points as possible. The round will end when the final line of the Flinch tune plays and the final jump-scare has popped.

During game play, the rules are simple:

1. The aim is to make other players flinch. A flinch is a physical reaction to a scare – a gasp, a jump, a shout, or running away.
2. A flinch can be obtained through any means, except physical contact. No touching.
3. When a flinch is obtained, the flincher must use the app to give a point to the player who scared them, simply by holding their mobile devices close together and clicking a button.

Failure to follow the rules will result in player elimination. The players with the most points will be rewarded with a coveted place on the Flinch leaderboard.

Do you have what it takes to scare your way to the top? There's only one way to find out . . .

CHAPTER ONE

THE GAME

A scream splits the silence of the Dread Wood. I brace myself against the tree behind me and force myself to be still. Not easy when my body feels like a human beehive. Under my skin everything is buzzing, vibrating, like I might explode at any moment, splattering blood and body parts across the green of the woods. I picture it for a second, and strangely enough the thought distracts me enough to calm me. The image leaves me with one lasting thought: I do not want to die at this school.

Quiet again. Time to move. I can't resist a quick glance above me and a scan of the ground ahead. The memory of the last time I was hunted in these woods will always be with me, but I remind myself that the spiders have been gone for months. I'm facing a different enemy now – fewer legs but almost as frightening.

I dart forward, keeping in the shadows as much as I can, avoiding the bright sunlight that streaks through the gaps between the trees. I reckon I know these woods better than most people, which gives me an advantage. There are places where I know people will be hiding – the hollowed-out bushes close to the paths which make everyone who finds them think they've discovered some massive secret, until they spot the screwed-up candy wrappers and left-behind bottles and cans. Someone will be huddling in there now, thinking they have the drop on whoever passes by. Easy target.

As I get close to one of the hollows, I see movement. It's too early in spring for everything in the woods to have properly filled out – shrubs are still budding, leaves uncurling. Through the tiny shoots of green, I can see a dark shape, crouching, shifting slightly on their feet like they can't keep still.

I hold back for a moment before I make my move. It could be a trap – someone acting as bait while an ally waits to pounce. That's the trouble with Flinch: you're never sure whether you're the hunter or the prey.

In the second before I attack, I hear something that stops me in my tracks. A squeak of fright that makes me peer into a hollowed-out bush, and then a hiss of disgust as the person hiding there brushes a bug off their clothes.

'Naira,' I say. 'You're lucky it's me who found you, otherwise you'd be flinched for sure.'

'Oh god, Angelo.' Naira looks out at me and holds up a hand for me to help her from the hollow. 'This bush is infested. Did you see that disgusting creature? What was it?'

'A beetle, I think.' I pull her under a branch

and out into the open. 'It was hard to tell, what with you being in a shadowy bush, and the creature being only a few millimetres long.'

'Small doesn't mean harmless,' Naira huffs, brushing invisible bugs off her PE kit. 'Just look at Hallie.'

I grin. 'We need to get out of here. Game's not over yet.'

'I'm coming with you,' Naira says, retying her ponytail. 'And don't look at me like that – I'd be perfect on my own, anywhere but in these woods.'

I nod, but I'm already looking forward to telling the others about this later and seeing the glare on her face. 'Let's go.' I lead her away from the path. She's strong, fast and stealthy, and I'm glad to have her at my back.

We jog further into the Dread Wood, only stopping now and again to look and listen.

Nobody knows exactly when Flinch became a thing, or who played the first game. We first heard about it a few weeks ago, through listening in on muttered chats in the dining hall between clustered groups of people hunched over pizza slices. Once it started being talked about in all the usual places online, there wasn't a person in the school who didn't know what it was or how to play. Everyone has the Flinch app on their phone, and once you have the app, it's in the rules that you have to play. I've always been good at breaking rules, but Flinch is so addictive that I've never even been tempted to swerve a round.

The rules are simple. The Flinch app notifies players at the start of a round by playing the start of a tune – *Half a pound of tuppenny rice, half a pound of treacle, that's the way the money goes* . . . Then the music pauses. In that time everyone scatters, hides, finds places to launch their attacks from. The aim is to make other players flinch or run away, usually by jump-scaring them, but everyone has their own technique. Physical contact isn't allowed, but other than that, anything is fair game. If you make someone flinch you connect the Flinch apps on your phones to claim your point. The round ends when the app plays the final line of the song.

'Do you have a plan?' Naira whispers. 'Surely nobody's going to be hiding this far in? I want to win, not get lost so deep in the woods that my body isn't located until I've been eaten by maggots.'

'We're going to circle back,' I say. 'I know another noob spot we can check out – bound to be someone lurking there.'

'Well, can we circle back soon? The round's going to end, I have won zero flinches today, and I'm starting to feel like I'm in the Hunger Games out here in all this nature.'

'Any sign of the others?' I spot the boundary fence through the trees – the place where the school grounds end but the Dread Wood goes on, past the train tracks, until it reaches the edge of town.

'If Hallie was close, I feel like I would have known instantly, so she must be over the other side of the woods . . .' Naira says. I nod – Hallie's game tactics involve less sneaking in for surprise attacks, and more shouting aggressively at people until they can't stand it any more and give her the flinch point.

'I heard a scream about five minutes ago that I'm pretty sure was Gus,' Nai carries on. 'I mean the pitch of it – you know how he sounds like a stepped-on puppy – it's distinct, you know?'

'It is,' I say. I hesitate, but I have to ask. 'What about Colette?'

I'm glad Naira is behind me so she can't see my cheeks burning. I know she knows anyway – I can picture her annoying expression, just like she can picture mine.

'I have no idea about Colette,' she says. 'You know how she is – for someone so apparently pure of heart, she's incredibly good at being sneaky.'

It's true that Colette is a lot of things all at once. I've never known anyone like her.

Naira, Gus, Hallie and me were forced

together last November during a Saturday detention that turned into a fight for our lives. In one day we went from being people who didn't even look at each other in the corridor to good friends. Over the past four months we've grown even closer, but there's still a lot we don't know about each other.

With Colette, things are even more complicated. The four of us were in detention that day because we'd treated her badly. Worse than badly. We'd been awful to her. Once detention was over, all we wanted to do was apologise. I never expected to be forgiven, but Colette being Colette, I was. We all were. And since then we've stuck together. Being part of a group is new for me – feels as uncertain as walking across the school field, wondering if there's something lying in wait under the ground. Like a trapdoor could open up beneath my feet.

Something stops me, suddenly. I don't know if I saw some movement in the corner of my eye, or my ears picked up the smallest sound, or if it was just a feeling, nothing specific, but my body tenses. I put a hand on Naira's shoulder, turn and meet her eyes, trying to warn her without speaking. I don't know if she senses it too, or if she gets my message loud and clear, but she freezes instantly. We stand shoulder to shoulder, not even breathing, watching the woods around us. The bees inside me thrum quietly, stingers ready. My whole body knows it: we're being watched.

'Where?' Naira says.

'Not sure,' I say. 'Behind, to the left maybe. I think there's someone there.'

I'm too focused, too alert. My eyes are staring so hard that they're blurring. All I see are tree trunks, every one different but at the same time somehow identical, murky, towering, twisting pillars, concealing a million things. I try to relax and breathe in through my nose – the moss and earth scent of the woods always soothes me – but I can't smell anything except the sting inside my nose as it sucks in the chill, damp air. The back of my neck is itching, and it takes everything in me not to scratch it like a bear against a tree trunk. I stare into the Dread Wood as branches creak and sway in the breeze. Maybe I can see the start of a silhouette behind a cluster of evergreens, but I could be imagining it.

In these woods, just a few months ago, we were hunted by genetically mutated giant spiders. I know it sounds impossible, insane, unreal. But it happened. And ever since then I've found that my senses are a bit more finely tuned, my nerves strained. And of course Flinch is only making it worse.

It's Naira who snaps me out of it. 'We should move,' she whispers. 'If there's someone there, they're going to follow, and then we'll know.'

I nod. We turn and walk on.

A twig snaps behind us, and my heart lurches. I feel Naira tense up, but we keep moving as if we haven't heard it. The best thing we can do is lure them in, so when the ambush comes, we're ready for it. I remind myself that it doesn't matter if someone jumps out, only that we stay strong and don't flinch.

Another snap – from the same direction, but closer. We keep moving, as casually as we can.

'We counter-attack,' Naira whispers. 'Wait till they think they have us, then turn and scream in their face. They'll get a shock, we'll get the flinch points.'

'Yeah,' I say. 'That could work. We'll have to get the timing right, though – save it for the last possible moment when they're practically upon us.'

So we walk, feeling someone at our backs, dying to run or turn around, but not wanting to lose. It's been a couple of minutes, and I've been so fixated on whoever is following us, that I haven't noticed where we're heading until we're there.

'Look where we are,' I sigh, stepping up on to a tree stump.

'Great. My favourite spot.' Naira looks up into the trees looming over us and shudders. We're in the clearing where the spider monsters attacked us. Three of them – Big Brown, Wolf Grey, Red Skull. It's where we fought for our lives, where we were impaled with toxic spines. I rub the spot on my shoulder where the biggest one hit me, and where the mark still shows on my skin.

'What is it that Gus calls it again?' Naira asks.

'The Arena of Eternal Horror.'

'Yeah, that works,' she sighs.

I realise that we've stopped walking. Neither of us wants to go through it.

'We do it here,' I say, as I hear the soft crunch of a footstep on the forest floor. So close now. 'Ready?'

She nods. 'Ready.'

Instead of saying it out loud, I use my fingers to count to three, holding the first one up where only Naira and I can see it.

One.

I take a deep breath in, ignore the itch on the back of my neck.

Two.

The breeze drops and it's like the warm breath of our ambusher take its place, grazing the top of my head from above. Whoever it is, they're tall. My mind flicks through the possibilities, trying to work out who it could be.

Three.

I try to brace myself inside without giving anything away on the outside, but at the same time, Naira spins around with a roar. I have less than a second to be frustrated at myself that I didn't make it clear we were going after three, not on three, before I join her, swearing out loud in a way that our teachers would be really disappointed about. But that second has made all the difference. I turn to see a figure running away from us into the trees, and Naira staring after them, pale-faced, looking like she's seen a ghost.

'Come on,' I say. 'They're running, you can

claim the flinch point.' I make to go after them, but Naira doesn't move.

'I wasn't expecting that,' she says, and her heart is beating so fast that I can see her sweatshirt fluttering on her chest. She swears.

'What?' I say, worrying now. 'What is it?'

She opens her mouth to answer, but a jarring sound suddenly blasts from our pockets and rings out across the Dread Wood and stops her. We both jump. It's the Flinch app, playing the end of the tune that lets us know the round is over.

Pop goes the weasel.

'That was intense,' I breathe.

'Angelo . . .' Naira grabs my wrist. 'I think–'

A noise in the clearing behind us makes us both whirl around. And what we see makes me turn cold. There's someone watching us from a few metres away. They're standing perfectly still, head tipped to one side, looking at us like we're rats in a science lab. I don't know for sure who it is because they're wearing a mask.

A creepy-ass rubber mask, covering their head and neck. Like some old-school killer-clown thing that would spring out of a jack-in-the-box – cracked white skin, painted eyes, fixed toothy grin, neon-yellow fluff for hair.

I don't know why they're looking at us.

'Round's over,' I shout. 'Didn't you hear?'

The masked figure doesn't move, doesn't speak. They hum, though, the tune for the end of the game. *Pop goes the weasel*.

I take a step towards them. I want to know who they are.

Then from behind us, back where the original stalker was, there's another sound that makes my blood feel like it's going to freeze. It's the tune again, but not hummed.

Whistled.

CHAPTER TWO

OUT OF THE WOODS

There's another masked person behind us. Taller, wider. Huge, really. A floor-to-ceiling fridge-freezer of a person. They whistle the tune again, slowly, from the start.

I look between the two figures: one small and thin, skeletal arms and legs showing through their dark clothes when the breeze blows against them. The other one: same mask, same clothes, four times the size. Whistling.

'It's them, isn't it?' Naira gasps.

I know exactly who she means. Mr and Mrs Latchitt. Dread Wood High's former caretakers who hated us so much that they set their spider monsters on us. And Colette's grandparents, though she's never met them and, as far as I know, never wants to. They're crazy intelligent, insanely creepy, and dead set on punishing us for treating Colette badly in the past.

She's forgiven us. They haven't.

The Latchitts disappeared after we blew up the spiders and their lab, but the chances of them coming back for a second chance at revenge are scarily not that low. I pull Naira back a step, to the side of the clearing where we escaped the spider attack, keeping the distance between us and them, one on each side. I don't know for sure it's the Latchitts, but I do know that I want to be far away from the Dread Wood.

'Do we fight, or do we run?' I say.

At my side, I see Naira shake her head.

Then two things happen to make up my mind. First I hear a sound from the woods between the two masked figures. Someone else whistling. And then a jolt as a high-speed train suddenly blasts its horn and comes tearing up the tracks behind the boundary fence. Nobody was expecting it, and in that split second of distraction, I grab Naira's hand and run back towards the field.

We pound through the trees, branches scratching at our faces and snagging on our clothes, but we don't stop or slow down. I swear I can feel that hot breath on the back of my head at every step, and part of me wants to turn and look over my shoulder. That would mean running smack into a tree though, and a broken face isn't going to help me right now. When I see the grass of the field ahead, I feel like the bees inside are individually going to combust. Naira is just ahead of me, and I focus on matching her pace, watching her ponytail swing like it can hypnotise me into making it out of these woods.

Finally, we erupt out of the Dread Wood and

on to the field, where the other Year 7s from the game are finding their mates, flopping down on to the grass to catch their breath and brag about their gameplay. None of them bother to look up as we pelt out of the trees – everyone's too tired, sinking into the energy dip that comes after each round.

We locate Hallie and Gus – I hear them before I see them, what with them being two of the loudest people in the whole school – and we run over to where they're sitting.

'You both heard it, right?' Hallie looks up. Out of everyone on the field, she looks the least like she's just been through an ordeal. A round of Flinch is like a night in a haunted house, or a ride on a rusty roller coaster – you're on edge the whole time, your mind plays tricks on you, and you have the fear lurking underneath it all that something could genuinely go horribly wrong, even if it is just a game. But Hal looks like she's just been walking puppies in the park – pink cheeks, face lit up, huge smile.

'Listen,' Naira says. 'We need to talk to you.'

'Wait.' Hallie holds her hand up. 'This is important. Did you, or did you not hear Gus screaming like a teen in a slasher movie?'

I glance back at the Dread Wood, looking for a flash of white mask or yellow hair. I see Naira doing the same. The trees are silent and still, looming and watching, giving nothing away. My legs are shaking, and I drop to the ground, sitting on the grass next to Hal and Gus, but making sure I have a clear view of the Dread Wood. I'm not ready to turn my back on it yet.

'What the hell's wrong with you two?' Gus looks from me to Nai and back again. Naira sits too, coming down like she's been shot out of the sky. 'You look like you've had your fully flinched butts handed to you on a dining-hall tray.'

'We saw something,' I say. 'In the woods.' I look around at the groups of Year 7s and see she's not there. I should have noticed sooner. 'Where's Colette?'

'Not back yet.' Hallie shrugs. 'She must have gone deep in or climbed a tree or something.'

Naira looks at me, but I can't quite read her eyes.

'We should look for her,' I say, heaving myself off the grass. 'The woods aren't safe.'

'No shiz, Angelo.' Gus rolls his eyes. 'They're full of pumped-up teens and broken glass.'

Being out here now and seeing everyone else so normal is making me doubt myself. I think back to the clearing and wonder if I was exaggerating things in my mind because of the adrenaline.

Naira huffs. She's had enough. 'We saw people in the woods, two of them, in creepy masks.'

'Ooh, masks are a good idea,' Gus says. 'It's not against the rules, right? I'm gonna try that next time.'

'You'll still lose,' Hallie snorts. 'Besides, masks are for cowards. If you're going to make someone scream, you want them to be seeing the triumph on your face as you claim your victory.'

21

'One of them was huge,' I say. 'Over six foot tall, built like a tank.'

'Probably a sixth-former doing a bit of Year 7 bullying,' Gus says. 'You know what those smug, suited, shiny-shoed thugs are like.'

'And that would explain the mask,' says Hallie. 'He wouldn't want to be identified.'

'He stalked us to the clearing,' Naira says. 'Where the other person was waiting.'

'Call the clearing by its proper name, please, Naira,' Gus says.

'Absolutely not,' she snaps. 'The other person was tiny, like their bones would break in a strong wind.'

'Puberty comes to us all at different times,' Gus says. 'And some of us are sensitive about that, so let's not be judgy.'

'She hummed the Flinch tune,' I say, knowing for sure as I say it that she definitely was a she.

'Guys, you are seriously paranoid. We all hum the Flinch tune all the time – it's like, constantly stuck in our heads,' Hallie says.

Gus nods. 'It's the new school anthem.'

'And the other guy whistled it,' Naira says. 'They stood there, staring at us, in the clearing . . .'

'Arena of Eternal Horror,' Gus coughs.

'She hummed, he whistled. They were enjoying it. Just like they did when they murdered chickens and left us to be eaten by spiders.' Naira looks at me. 'Right?'

'Yeah,' I say.

'So wait.' Hallie is finally looking at least a *little* worried. 'You think it was *them*?'

'Felt like it at the time,' I say. 'But there was someone else there too. I heard another person whistling.'

Gus whacks me on the arm. 'Can't have been them then. The Latchitts work in a two-person team. And I say two *people* because I'm not including their weird monster army in this. Unless one of the spiders made it out of the explosion and has learned to whistle, it doesn't fit.'

'Maybe,' I say, because I'm questioning everything now.

'Just an overly body-sprayed sixth-former and an under-developed Year 7 – who we are not being mean about because my mum says we all fill out when the time is right – forming an unlikely alliance to freak people out in the scariest spot in the wood. The Arena of Eternal Horror claims another victim.' Gus gives himself a fist bump.

'I really do hate to agree with the person who screams like a fake-tanned try-hard finding out she hasn't been voted prom queen in a teen movie,' Hallie says. 'But Gus is right. There are way more likely explanations for what happened than that the Latchitts have come back to join in a game with a bunch of high-schoolers. Someone was messing with you. Sit your paranoid butt down.'

'And look, here's Colette.' Gus waves as Colette jogs out of the woods and comes running over to us, looking tired and flushed but not like she's just had the biggest scare of her life. I let my body relax back into the grass as it floods with relief.

'Hey.' She grins as she plops down next to me. 'Anyone score any flinch points?'

Hallie, Gus, Naira and I all exchange a look. We're not going to mention the Latchitts in front of Colette unless we have to. Her psycho grandparents are a bit of an awkward subject.

'I got three.' Hallie smiles. 'Angelo?'

'Just the one,' I say.

'I'm going to beat you if you're not careful.' Colette looks pretty pleased with herself. 'I got four.'

'Colette, you are ninety per cent Disney princess, and ten per cent world's most deadly assassin,' Gus says. 'And that makes you an expert Flinch player. How'd you do, Naira?'

'None for me this time,' Naira says. 'The Dread Wood makes me sub-optimal. I'll redeem myself on the next round.'

Colette looks at Gus and wrinkles her nose.

'I have to ask . . .'

'Yes, it was him screaming like a kid who's climbed out of a river to find a leech on his boy parts in a coming-of-age movie,' Hallie says.

'Oh man!' Gus says. 'That's so triggering.'

Colette puts her arm around him. 'I think it's sweet that you're so bad at Flinch. And you have many other skills. Like freestyle rap and turning your eyelids inside out.'

'That's true,' Gus sniffs. 'I'm not mad because I'm bad at Flinch, though. I'm mad because the scream I was shooting for was curly-haired-burglar-takes-tarantula-to-the-face-in-Christmas-movie. If I'm going to scream multiple times a day, I want to channel the best.'

We all laugh, and some of the worry eases away. We're all here, we're all fine, and Hallie's right – there are more likely explanations for what happened in the woods.

Dread Wood High is the perfect setting for getting creeped out. Part of the school is an old mansion house, with stags' heads on the walls, creaky, narrow stairways with stained-glass windows, and a rumoured ghost. The school grounds are enormous and include ornamental gardens, farm animals and the stretch of the Dread Wood leading up to the train tracks. It's easy to get carried away with imaginary horror scenarios.

'Canton's coming,' someone shouts, and people start picking up their bags and casually scattering.

I can't quite find the motivation to get off the grass yet.

Mr Canton, our head of year, jogs over to the thirty or so of us who still haven't moved. 'What's happening over here? Year 7 picnic and I wasn't invited?' He stops and smiles around at everyone, slightly out of breath, his tie flapping in the breeze.

There's a few seconds of silence when everyone just stares at him. The first rule of Flinch is that nobody talks about it to anyone who's likely to shut it down.

'Just chilling, sir,' someone says eventually.

'Ah, chilling, hanging out, sharing some bantz.' Mr C nods. I can't see the face of every person sitting on that field, but I'm confident they're all making the same expression that we are. 'Nothing like rolling with your homies, am I right?'

Nobody speaks.

'As happy as I am to see you all getting on so well,' Mr Canton says, 'the second bell is about to ring and you have a long walk across the field to registration. So if you're going to make it in time, it might be an idea to get moving.' He acts like he doesn't notice the eye-rolling and under-breath insults as people start picking themselves off the grass and moving towards the school building.

Colette stands and holds out a hand to pull me up. Hallie and Gus are on their feet too, but Naira's still sitting. I offer her a hand.

'Ah, my favourite hashtag "Back On Trackers"!' Mr Canton walks over to us. 'Glad to see you're all steaming ahead now. Although not across this field, obviously.' He winks at us. 'Our Saturday session was the making of you all. You took the opportunity . . .' he holds his hands out, 'and you grabbed it and ran with it.' He mimes catching some kind of imaginary ball, tucking it under his arm and running on the spot. I'm glad the other Year 7s are ahead of us now, because it's more than a bit embarrassing. Mr Canton smiles. 'I'm so proud of you.'

'Oh god, sir, you're not going to cry, are you?' Hallie says.

Mr Canton sniffs. 'Nothing wrong with shedding a few tears, Hallie. We should all feel free to openly express our thoughts and emotions.'

We pick up the pace. Mr Canton walks with us.

'And you know that I am always here for you. We went through a stressful experience together. I know the police weren't convinced, but both you and I know that there was more going on that day than a random sinkhole that sucked me underground and then magically resealed itself. I was definitely hit on the head, and we are still missing a piglet. Situations like that aren't easy to get over. They reverberate through our lives in unexpected ways.'

'Are you having nightmares again, Mr C?' Gus says. And we all laugh, even Mr Canton.

'LOL,' he says with a grin. We cringe. 'But seriously though, guys. It's hashtag "OK Not To Be OK". My office door is always open if you feel like you need to tell me anything.'

The second bell saves us from having to respond to that. Mr Canton bolts off after a couple of stragglers he has spotted kicking a ball in the tennis courts. Gus and Hal go back to arguing about the scream, while Colette shrieks with laughter. Naira and I follow behind, and my thoughts return to what happened in the woods. I look across at Nai, wondering what she's thinking, but my eyes dart away when I see something dancing in my peripheral vision –

a speck of neon yellow blowing past Colette's shoulder. But I blink, and it's gone, and I'm left not knowing if it was there at all.

CHAPTER THREE

POSSESSED

We go round Hallie's after school. She lives on one of the nice roads opposite the church, with the boasty kind of houses that have an extra bedroom just for if a friend comes to stay. Everything's tidy inside, and the cupboards are always full of food. And there's space, and light. You can stretch out and breathe without being in anyone's way. It's a world away from our flat on the estate, where you can't sit down without planting your ass on top of something that shouldn't be there but has nowhere else to go.

I'm not complaining, though. Hallie's parents let us come over whenever we want, and they always feed us.

'It's so good you don't have to go straight home after school any more,' Colette says, trying to balance five cans of Coke Zero and two giant bags of posh crisps in her arms while walking slowly towards the back door.

'You're going to drop those,' I say. 'You want me to take something?'

'Nah, I have it completely under control.' She squints through her glasses at the snacks and I gently steer her away from the corner of the counter she's about to walk into.

'Yeah, it's made a big difference, Raph getting into after-school club. No more rushing back to babysit.'

I'm close to my little brother. Mostly because I've always looked after him while my parents worked, and grabbed a few hours of sleep between shifts, and tried to pay for the flat for us to live in and food in the fridge. It was the only way I could help.

'You miss it.' Colette glances up at me. 'Don't you?'

I nod. 'A bit. We've always spent so much time together and I guess I liked being his best buddy. Now all he talks about is some kid he met at club called Kenzie who is apparently smarter, braver and more buff than I am. I almost feel jealous. Is that stupid?'

'Nope,' Colette says with a smile. 'It's cute. And you know, he'll always love you the most, even if you're not as buff as Kenzie.'

I open the back door for her and she walks through, just about managing not to trip on the step.

'But,' I say, 'he has friends, and club feeds him his bodyweight in fruit. He's happy.'

'And it means you can hang out with us.' Colette looks at me over the top of her glasses, which are sliding down her nose. 'At least until Kenzie's old enough to replace you here too.'

I push the glasses up for her. 'And I can look

after the well-being pigs twice a week,' I say. 'That's the best part.'

'Charming. Bring on the Kenzie years.'

'Hurry up, I'm literally dying of thirst here,' Hallie shouts over to us from the – get this – *garden sofas*. Yeah, they even have sofas in the garden, with a dining table and a built-in fire pit.

Colette half places, half drops the cans and crisps on the table, and we take a seat, everyone grabbing at the Coke before it rolls on to the floor.

Gus opens one of the bags of crisps and shoves a handful into his mouth. 'Aah,' he sighs mid-crunch. 'You can tell these aren't from the value range.' He slumps back in his seat and crunches away with a big smile on his face. 'You know it's quality if it says "artisan" on the packet.'

'What even is artisan?' Hallie says.

'I don't know for sure,' Gus answers. 'But I think it has something to do with windmills and flat caps, and not working on Sundays. Who even cares when it tastes this good?'

'So are we still on for the fair on Friday?' I ask.

'Hell, yes,' Hallie says.

'I guess,' says Naira.

I look at her. 'You don't sound excited.'

She shrugs. 'It's just a travelling fair – lame rides that look like they're going to fall apart, a load of games that are rigged so you can't win, every idiot from school running around being a moron . . .'

'Oh no, no, Naira.' Gus holds his hand up. 'The Finches Green fair is not just a travelling fair. It's a Dread Wood High rite of passage. Twice a year they ride into town, bringing with them the stuff our dreams are made of. A night of risk-taking. A night of freedom and fun. A night of staring Lady Luck down the barrel of her RPG and saying, "You wanna take me on? Bring it, I'm ready for you." And then they're gone, rolling away like the morning mist.'

We're all cracking up. Even Naira.

'And because they're only open to Dread

Wood students on Friday, my parents are letting me go.' Colette grins. 'They figure it's safe enough if it'll be supervised by teachers.'

'They clearly haven't spent enough time with our teachers,' Hallie snorts. 'It's going to be chaos.'

'You'll have us, though, Col,' I say. 'We'll stay together the whole time.'

'Mum figures that a school-supervised event is the last place the Latchitts will show their faces, if they are still around,' Colette says. 'Everyone at Dread Wood knows who they are. If they're spotted, the police will want to talk to them straight away.'

'Your mum thinks they'll be back?' Naira asks.

'I don't think she knows what to think. She ran away from them when she was seventeen, but she's still terrified of them. Since I told her about what happened to you guys in November, she's become paranoid. I catch her looking over her shoulder sometimes, like they might be watching her.'

'Did she say why she never told you about them?' Hallie asks.

Colette shrugs. 'I haven't asked her. Or about who my dad is. She went through something traumatic, and her way of dealing with it is to block it out. I don't want to upset her.'

'It's your right, though,' Hallie says. 'Not knowing would kill me. I'd have to ask.'

'I used to think about it,' says Colette. 'But I love my mum, and she's given me everything I've ever needed and wanted. I used to think she was a bit weird, needing security cameras covering every centimetre of the house, and I noticed her watching me like a stalker at soft play while the other parents went for a coffee and a chat. And the thing with the sealed envelopes revealing the location of a concealed weapons stash to be opened in the event of her disappearance was, like, a bit bizarre. But I figured she had her reasons.'

'Shut up – you have access to a secret weapons stash?' Gus says, more excited than he was even about the artisan crisps.

Colette sniggers. 'Course not, you twerp. Well, not that I know of anyway. But finding out about the Latchitts has given me so many answers about why she acts the way she does.'

'Are you worried about them coming for you?' I ask, trying not to sound like I think she should be worried about them coming for her.

'Nah.' She smiles. 'My mum's taught me to be ready. To be willing to do whatever it takes to survive. Whether that's lying, fighting, running away, or writing a song about my feelings.'

'And now that we know about the Latchitts, Dread Wood High is actually the safest place you could be.' Hallie slurps her Coke with a grin.

I'm not so sure. Like Col's mum, I've never properly been able to my guard down since what happened to us all. The masked figures in the woods have only made me more on edge.

'So we're going to the fair, and we're going to have the time of our lives,' Gus says. 'Even Naira.'

We're jolted out of our conversation by our phones, singing out the Flinch tune in perfect sync. *Half a pound of tuppenny rice* . . . It's the start of a new round.

Gus drops the crisps and jumps out of his seat, looking around at the rest of us like we're a pack of hyenas moving in for the kill. Naira's half out of her seat too, poised and ready. Colette is trying to act casual but I can see the tension in her jaw as she clamps her teeth together. I slowly put down my can of Coke.

'Guys,' Hallie says. She's still sitting, choosing a crisp from the bag in her hand. 'Chill out for god's sake. I love Flinch as much as the rest of the world, but we're sitting this round out.'

'But we can't,' Gus gasps. 'We have to play. It's the rules.'

I feel the bees start up inside me again. It's like as soon as that tune plays, my body's being wound up like a jack-in-the-box, tighter and tighter. My whole body is tingling. And the back of my neck is itching like there are fire ants crawling all over it.

'Since when did we care about some random person's rules?' Hallie asks.

'Naira cares,' Gus says. 'We should play.'

'No, the old Naira cared,' Hallie says, holding a crisp up to the light to inspect it. 'We all agreed after detention that our own rules come before anyone else's. Ugh, a green bit . . .' She flings the crisp away. 'And what did we agree when we started playing Flinch?'

'That we would never flinch each other,' I said. I know we agreed that, and yet my body is itching to play.

'So sit down and eat artisan crisps. Nobody's going to know if we sit this one out.' Hallie, the most hot-headed person I know, is telling the rest of us to calm down.

We look at each other for a second or two, and then I pick up my Coke again. Gus shuffles back on to the sofa. Naira slides back into her place. Colette takes a deep breath.

There's a thud and a squawk from the end of Hallie's garden.

'Was that your chicken?' Naira asks.

'Yeah.' Hallie makes a face and puts down the crisps, listening. 'I wonder what's up with her?'

I freeze, mid-chew, and we all lean forward on our seats, straining our ears. Then there's another noise from Michelle's enclosure. It's loud, urgent, somewhere between a scream and a bark, repeating over and over. We run down the lawn to the henhouse, which is tucked behind a semicircle of trees and shrubs. I expect to see a predator run off as we round the corner. A cat, or maybe a fox if it's hungry enough to venture out early. But there's just Michelle.

'Is that normal?' Gus asks.

Michelle is hopping from one leg to the other, using the raised leg to claw at herself with her foot. She's viciously attacking herself anywhere she can reach. Feathers are flying. She's bleeding. Then she starts throwing herself at the side of her henhouse, hard enough to crack bones from the look of it.

Hallie swears and starts fumbling with the latch of the enclosure.

'Are you sure you should go in there?' Colette says. 'She could hurt you.'

Hallie rolls her eyes and lifts the latch.

'I'll help,' I say, moving to the door. The others step back, their faces pale, looking horrified.

We ease into the enclosure and I shut the door behind me. Michelle has stopped hammering her house and is using her beak to pull out her feathers – yanking them from the roots like they're poison, and flinging them away.

'Hey, Mimi,' Hallie says, taking a step towards her. 'What's going on?'

I move to the opposite side of the enclosure so that I can grab Michelle if she runs from Hallie. Michelle doesn't seem to have even noticed us. She keeps gouging away at herself with her claws and beak.

'It's like she's possessed,' Gus says.

Hallie moves closer and crouches down. 'It's OK, Mimi, calm down. Calm down.' She reaches out an arm towards Michelle, and the chicken finally notices her, launching herself into the air with a shriek. 'Why isn't she coming to me? She always comes to me.'

'We just need to grab her,' I say. 'Someone get a towel from the house to wrap her in. Hal, try to get her backed up against the henhouse in the far corner.'

But Michelle isn't playing. She dodges us, runs, lashes out even. She smashes herself against the wire of the enclosure and I can see at least five places where she's bleeding. We're trying to be gentle because we don't want to hurt her. It isn't working.

'I have the towel, Angelo,' Colette says. 'I'll pass it in.' She opens the door just wide enough to get her arm through, with her sweatshirt sleeve pulled down to cover her hand. She's scared, I realise. Of a chicken. Even worse,

I realise I am a bit too. I've never seen anything like this. Hallie is crying.

We struggle on for a few more minutes, until our phones ring out for the end of the Flinch round that we had completely forgotten about. It makes all of us jump, and startles Michelle, and in that few seconds of distraction, I manage to grab her in the towel, wings pinned down tight so she can't get away.

'I'll take her,' Hallie says, and I pass the chicken-towel bundle over to her. Michelle has gone limp. Hallie has a jagged scratch across her cheek but she doesn't seem to notice. 'I need to get her to the vet.'

'Do you have a box thing to put her in?' Gus asks.

'In the shed,' Hallie says.

'On it.' Gus runs off.

'I'll get your mum.' Naira's already sprinting towards the house.

Colette puts her arm around Hal's shoulder and squeezes gently. 'She'll be OK,' she says, then she looks up at me. 'Won't she, Angelo?'

I hesitate. I don't know if she will be OK. There's clearly something badly wrong with Michelle to make her act that way. When Gus said she seemed possessed, he wasn't being overly dramatic. Obviously I don't believe in evil spirits, or any of that, but it was like Michelle had fully lost control of her brain. And I hate lying – I don't think it helps to give people false hope. So I go with, 'Whatever's wrong, I'm sure the vet will work out what it is. You'll be able to get some answers.'

Gus is back with the box, followed by Naira with Hallie's mum, and three minutes later, they're in the car on the way to the vet, leaving me, Gus, Naira and Colette sitting on the wall at the front of Hallie's house.

'Don't they say that birds are evolved from dinosaurs?' Colette asks. 'For the first time in my life, I can totally see it.'

'Yeah,' I say. I'm thinking about the Latchitts again – how they genetically modified the spiders to turn them into creatures that shouldn't exist.

'You saw dinosaur, I saw full demonic possession.' Gus puts his hands in his pockets. 'Michelle doesn't need a vet, she needs a priest.'

Naira doesn't say anything.

Colette's mum pulls up five minutes later. The worry on her face breaks into a smile as she sees us and waves. Colette eases herself off the wall and picks up her backpack. 'You guys want a lift home?'

'I'll take one,' Gus says. 'I'm done like a burnt roast potato.'

'We'll walk,' Naira says, pulling me up before I can answer. 'Won't we, Angelo?' She flashes me a Naira glare.

'Looks like it,' I say.

Colette raises an eyebrow, but shrugs and says, 'OK, see you tomorrow.'

'Careful on the mean streets of Finches Heath,' Gus calls back, as he heads to the car.

And then they're gone.

'You want to explain?' I ask Naira, as we put our backpacks on our backs and start trudging up the road.

'We need to talk,' she says. 'I'm not ready to pretend what happened at school was nothing.'

I sigh. I get it, but I also know that what the others said made sense. 'We could have overreacted. We were high on adrenaline. It was an intense situation.'

'We were scared, Angelo. Both of us. And we're not people who get scared easily.'

I don't mention the beetle in the bush from earlier.

We walk a moment without talking, both of us thinking.

'And what about Colette?' Naira asks. 'She didn't come out of the woods until way after everyone else. Where was she all that time? She never really said.'

'You know what she's like,' I said. 'She's always looking at the world around her, seeing stuff that's interesting, or beautiful, or whatever.' It's one of the things I like most about her. 'She probably stopped to take fifty photos of a gnarled tree.'

'Then why didn't she say so?'

'I don't know, because she thought we'd laugh at her?'

'But Colette doesn't mind being laughed at,' Naira says.

I side-eye Naira, and I don't like the expression on her face. 'What are you getting at?' I say. 'You're obviously thinking something bad about Colette – you might as well say it.'

'I'm thinking,' Naira snaps, 'about that third person outside the clearing. The one whistling. The one who joined in with whatever that horror show was, put on to weird us out.'

'You think that was Colette?' I stop walking, I'm so mad. 'No way, Naira. Just no way. You heard what she said about her mum and that whole situation. As if she'd join forces with her weird-ass grandparents!'

Naira rolls her eyes. 'We don't know Colette that well. She's clever. She's good at playing the cutesy quirky card. We don't know where she was during that round, and she has psychotic tendencies running through her family gene pool.'

'That's not fair and you know it, Nai. You can't judge people by their families. Colette is the kindest person I've ever known.'

'You don't think you're a bit blind to her faults because of what happened between you?' Naira says. 'You still feel bad for what you did to her at the start of Year 7, and you're so grateful for her forgiveness that you might not be seeing things clearly.'

I think about it for a second. Yeah, what I did to Colette – stealing from her to buy food for my brother, because I couldn't bear to admit how bad my family situation was – was the worst thing I ever did. I hadn't expected her to forgive me, and I promised myself when she did that I would never let her down again. But that doesn't mean I'm wrong now.

'Yeah, I am grateful,' I say. 'But I'm not an idiot. I'm a good judge of character, always have been, otherwise we wouldn't be standing here now.'

'Meaning we have you to thank for saving us all, I suppose?' Naira fumes. 'I seem to remember surviving the detention being a team effort.'

I open my mouth to snap back, but instead I stop. Take a breath. I know Colette wouldn't do anything to scare us, but I also know Naira wouldn't be saying all this just to be nasty. It's a misunderstanding, that's all, and I'm overreacting.

'I'm sorry, Nai,' I say. 'It's been a weird day, with the game, and with Michelle. We're stressed and tired and we're not going to make the best decisions right now.'

'But—' Naira says.

'I hear you, all right?' I say. 'Things feel off. Flinch was weird, and I can't stop replaying Michelle's . . . whatever that was, in my mind. I've never seen or heard of anything like it, and

I guess I'm wondering if something nasty's been done to her. She used to belong to the Latchitts, remember? Maybe they messed with her like they did with the spiders. Let's talk again tomorrow when we've had a chance to rest. I promise I'll keep an open mind.'

Naira bites her lip, and nods.

We start walking again, chatting like normal, but there's an edge underneath it all. Naira's wrong about Colette – I know that, no question. But I think she's right that there's something going on. I scan our surroundings constantly, waiting for something bad to happen. And though the rest of the walk home is same old normal, I can't shake the feeling of wrongness. It feels like something's lurking, just out of sight, waiting to tear everything apart.

CHAPTER FOUR

CHICKEN DINNER

We meet in the dining hall at morning break. It's an enormous old block of a room close to the mansion, with high ceilings that make it taller than it is wide. I don't think it's had any work done to it since it was built, so you can see every scar from over the years – the floor more scuff than tile; the walls a map of cracks; pillars with literal chunks missing from them like they've taken blast damage during the war. It's so full of holes that on a windy day you can't put your food down on the table without keeping a hand on it, or it will get caught in a draft and end up on the floor. The tables and benches are packed so close together that it's a mission to make your way from one side to the other. But if you can look past all that, you'll see the shiny counters that hold the finest heated-up processed food you could ever wish for. And that is why it's one of my favourite places in the school.

It's a cold, wet day, more like November than March, with the added shiz-dump that I don't have a coat because it's supposed to be spring. The hall is loud, too many people packed in because they don't want to be outside, and extra competition for the best food Dread Wood High has to offer.

The good stuff always runs out by halfway down the queue. I have enough credit on my lunch account for a sausage roll, but I got out of geography late and I can feel the pastry slipping away as I edge towards the counters. If I miss out, I'm blaming Mr Canton for getting so excited about the impact of human processes on the natural landscape.

'Angelo!' Colette's voice hollers above the clatter around me. She's waving from a bench at the far wall. 'We saved you a seat.'

I point at the serving hatch to show I'm holding on for my sausage roll, but Colette holds up something wrapped in a napkin and grins. 'Got you one.'

I ditch the queue, and the poor losers who almost definitely won't be getting their hot, buttery pastry fix, and edge through the crowds to where the others are sitting. There's an added level of noise and excitement in the hall – everyone eating their food as fast as they can in case a round of Flinch starts. Ready to jump up and run as soon as they hear that tune.

Hallie's stuffing a vegan wrap in her mouth, so aggressively that she's dropping bits of unidentifiable green down her blazer.

'You OK?' I say.

She nods and swallows. 'Couldn't eat dinner yesterday, because I felt sick about Michelle.'

I sit down on my saved seat, happy for the pocket of warmth between my friends. 'So what did the vet say?'

'She's stable and comfortable. She had a quiet night resting, and none of her injuries are as bad as they looked.'

Colette passes me the sausage roll, and I'm so grateful I could cry. 'Thanks, Col, you're the actual best.' I take a bite and let out a happy sigh. It is a thing of beauty. 'She hasn't, erm, freaked out again?' I say to Hallie, through a mouthful of buttery pastry.

'What Angelo is asking,' Gus says, 'is does the demonic entity that lives within her still plan on using her to rip us all to pieces?'

'Gus!' Naira says.

'What?' Gus lifts the lid of his burger and carefully squirts two packets of mayo in a complicated pattern over the meat. 'Clearly the chickapocalypse has begun. First Michelle, then the rest of them. RIP the human race.'

'Gus, tell me you didn't get a chicken burger.' Colette peers down at Gus's food. 'You did, didn't you?'

'Someone needs to take on the evil chickens.' Gus shrugs. 'Just doing my bit to save the world.' He takes a bite. 'Plus the chicken burgers here are so good. They must be artisan chickens.'

'Too soon for chicken jokes, Gus,' Naira says, offering me a sip of her hot chocolate.

Six months ago, I would never have accepted food from people at school. The thought would make me curl up inside. I honestly preferred to go hungry. It's different now though, with these guys – it doesn't feel like pity. When I have extra cash, I get them stuff back, and although I know I get more than I can give, I spend the nights when I can't sleep thinking about all the ways I'm going to balance things out in the future. I grin at Naira and take a swig of hot chocolate. So good.

'She's *not* possessed,' Hallie huffs. 'The vet thinks there must be a medical issue, so she's running tests today. We should know more later.'

'Blood tests and stuff?' I ask.

'Yeah, and a scan,' Hal says. 'Hopefully they won't find anything awful.'

Gus's whole face lights up and he opens his mouth to talk, but Naira holds up a finger. 'No, Gus. No.'

'But, I was just thinking—'

'They're not going to find a demon in Hallie's chicken,' Naira says.

Gus gasps. 'You were thinking it too!'

'Only because I always know what you're thinking.' Naira knocks back the rest of her drink.

'Will you get to see the scan, Hal?' Gus asks. 'Asking for . . . reasons.'

'She's not possessed,' Hallie says. She looks tired and paler than usual, but I can see she's trying not to smile.

'Nah, no, I know,' Gus says. 'But, just in case.'

Me, Naira and Colette groan, and Hallie throws her screwed-up food wrapper at Gus. It pings off his forehead and bounces on to the floor.

'I'm doing this for the future of the human race,' Gus sighs, taking a massive bite of his burger. 'You'll all be thanking me when there's one less murderous chicken rampaging through the school.'

'You're all staying for performance prep later, right?' Naira asks.

'Smooth subject change, Nai,' Hallie says.

'Yeah, well, someone's got to get Gus to shut his mouth about chickens.'

'I'm staying,' Colette says. 'I'm painting scenery in the art rooms. How 'bout you?'

'Naira's going to be practising her lines,' Gus snorts. 'It's gonna be tough to memorise those – what is it, Naira? – thirty words you have in the show.'

'At least I got a part,' Naira sniffs. She'd wanted the lead, but we've all heard her singing.

'I *could* have got a part, if I'd auditioned,' Gus says. 'A big one.'

'Sure you could,' Naira says.

'I'd rather die than audition for a school play,' Hallie says.

'Funny, 'cos you're the biggest drama queen I know,' I say. But I know what she means. I can't think of many things I'd hate more than auditioning or being in the Year 7 play. Unfortunately, participation is mandatory – we all have to work on it in some way.

'I'm on props in the drama stores,' I say. I look at Gus. 'What are you doing?'

'General assist,' he says, like he couldn't be more proud. 'My life has peaked.'

Hallie snorts. 'So you'll be running around fetching stuff like a stray dog.'

'And you?' Gus raises an eyebrow.

'Costume racks,' she sighs. 'I have to sort through them and pull out what needs cleaning and repairing.'

'We truly are the stars of Dread Wood High,'

Gus grins. And we all laugh.

'There are so many better things to be doing with our time,' I say, and I find myself thinking longingly of the pig yard where the school pigs will be hanging out, snuffling, chilling and living their best lives. I always loved spending time there, but I feel even closer to them since we rescued them from the killer spiders. Especially Klaus, who stares into my soul and seems to understand me better than most people I know. Apart from this lot.

'I don't know,' Colette says. 'I get to paint the wisteria growing up the balcony wall today. I've been looking forward to that.'

'OMG, the excitement,' Gus says, as the bell rings and we start getting our stuff together. 'Brace yourselves, guys. We're in for the wildest night of our lives.'

CHAPTER FIVE

JUNK AND DUST

Time moves differently when you're constantly on edge, waiting for something to happen. No one has any idea when the next round of Flinch will start, or which players will be selected. I've tried searching for patterns, so I can predict when I'll get the alert, but it mostly seems random. The only thing I know for sure is that the group of players will be people who are in close proximity at that moment. I spend half my time looking around me, watching and assessing the people nearby, deciding who'll be a hider, a runner, a lurker. Who'll thug it out, who'll ally up, who wants it the most.

When the bell rings at the end of the day, my rush of joy at being able to leave English and head out of school is slammed back down when I remember performance prep. I consider ditching. Six months ago, I would have ditched. But I promised my parents and Mr C that I'll be doing my best to stay out of detention, and I meant it. The next detention I get, I want to be for something really worthwhile. Besides, the others will be there. We might even get to hang out a bit.

'You're going to the arts block too?' Hallie shoves through half the class towards me.

I don't even bother answering, just make a face.

'I know, right?' Hallie says. 'I complained to the school council that enforced extra-curricular activities are an infringement of our rights as individuals, but they just pulled out the student charter and jabbed their oppressed fingers at some weak-ass points about fully participating in all aspects of school life. Full of loopholes and contradictions. It would never stand up in court.'

'You should be head of the student council,' I say. 'You sound forty years old when you talk like that. And I mean that in a nice way.'

'Nah, I'm too much of a loose cannon,' she says with a grin. 'They couldn't handle me.'

We head down the stairs of the classroom block. Hallie checks her messages for any news about Michelle.

'They haven't found anything wrong yet,' she says. 'They've looked "in all the usual problem areas", whatever that means, and there's nothing that shouldn't be there. They're going to sedate her tomorrow so they can do a full scan.' She sighs. 'Want to ditch this performance shiz and visit Klaus? I'm so not in the mood.'

'I'd love to,' I say. 'But–'

'I know, I know, we're saving our bad-kid points up for when we really need them. But if they're going to force us to stay after school, we should at least be allowed to choose what we do. Not everyone wants to be a freaking celebrity when they grow up.'

We step out into the grounds, which are grey with gloom from the rumbling storm clouds overhead. It feels later than it is.

'I swear it always rains here,' Hallie says. 'It's like the school of doom.'

'There's Colette.' I say.

Colette waits for us by the main door of the arts block. Most of Year 7 is heading for the main hall and green room where rehearsals take place. I imagine Naira standing in the corner, angrily muttering her lines over and over, and wishing she'd got a better part. There are probably thirty or so kids slouching into the arts block, including us at the back.

And of course it's Mr Canton standing in the entrance, ticking everyone's names off a list.

'Are you stalking us, Mr C?' Hallie says. 'You're not even an arts teacher.'

'I think of geography as an art.' Mr C's face lights up. 'But as head of year, overseeing your Year 7 performance is my responsibility. One of the delights of the job, if you will.'

'I'm glad someone's enjoying it,' I say. I really don't want to be here.

Mr C looks up from his clipboard. 'I know music and drama isn't for everyone, Angelo, but what this is really about is being part of a team effort. Your role here . . .' he scans the notes again, 'of . . . what is it you're doing?'

'Finding junk from a list and wiping the dust off it,' I say.

'Ah, yes.' He nods, with more enthusiasm than anyone should have at 3.30 p.m. on a school day when they're still at school. 'Your task is just as vital to the overall success of the performance as the part of the lead actors belting out their solos on the stage.'

Me, Colette and Hallie all snigger then,

because even Mr C can't believe that.

'It's true!' He looks sincere, but then says a little too quickly, 'Right, I must be off on my rounds to check everyone else in. Miss Heeps is working in her office by the main music room if you need her. Now onwards to your tasks!' He does a dramatic salute and starts walking off. 'Just a minute.' He stops and sniffs the air. 'Do you smell that?'

Hallie and Colette look as confused as I feel. I wonder for a second if I stepped in something bad.

'Yes, it's definitely . . .' Mr C sniffs again, 'the scent of teamwork in the air. There's no better smell. Get it in your nostrils, guys.'

We all groan. 'Mr C, you're so weird,' Hallie says. He laughs and gives us a backwards wave as he walks out of the door.

'Better get started, I suppose.' Hallie rolls her eyes. 'I'll come up and find you in a bit.' She turns right through a double door towards the textile stores.

Colette and I head for the stairs and start climbing.

Everything in the arts block is laid out in circles around an atrium – all inter-connected through narrow hallways and heavy doors. The stairs are in the centre, at the back, and lead up to two more floors, which look over the space in the middle. Music and textiles are downstairs.

Most times when you walk in, it's to the scraping of violins and bang of drums. The first floor has the drama rooms and some design stores. Top floor is art. There aren't enough windows here (some rooms don't have any at all) so it's dull and grim, even with every centimetre of wall space being covered in murals and artwork. Paper sculptures hang overhead – made-up creatures with human faces, and some steampunk hot-air balloon that looks like it will come crashing down at any second. Unnecessary pillars are everywhere – I think only there to display more art.

I'd give anything to be outside where I can

see all around me, and breathe in the smell of the trees. One day I'll travel the world, sleep outside every night and be as far away from buildings like this as I can.

'See you in a bit,' I say to Colette when we reach the first floor. She smiles, but it's flat and dim like the vibe in this building – not her usual goofy smile – and she carries on up the stairs. I feel it too, an overcast dreariness, like the storm clouds have followed us inside. I can't put my finger on why.

I push through the doors covered in posters from Dread Wood High shows through the years, and into the main drama room. Someone else has been here already – the lights are on, and I hear the creak of a door somewhere ahead of me. I don't call out, because I'm ninety-nine per cent sure that whoever it is, I don't want to be making awkward small talk with them.

I head to the next room, which is one of the only parts of the block that doesn't have scrat all over the walls. They're black in here, for some pretentious drama reason, I guess. There are huge wooden blocks that you can slide around to make different stages so I dump my bag on one of those and grab the clipboard that's been left on the desk in the corner. It has a list of props needed for the performance. My job is to dig through all the dusty junk in the cupboard, find them and clean them up.

I hear the slow tread of footsteps from the floor above me, creaking across the wooden boards, and the bang of a distant door being slammed.

The prop stores are more of a room than a cupboard. I go out of a side door in the black room, into a lift-sized passageway that's been painted with glow-in-the-dark squiggles and slashes. There's no natural light or air and it feels like somewhere a pretentious vampire would sleep. I hate it. On the right again, there are two steps leading down to a door that you probably wouldn't notice if you didn't know it was there. I creak it open. It's pitch-black inside.

The light switches are on the left, and I flick them up, waiting for the yellow strip lights to whir into action before I step into the room. I don't get scared easily, but there's no denying that this place is creepy when there's no one else around. I prop the door open with a bucket of wooden swords and start looking up and down the packed racks of props for anything from the list.

There are rows and rows of shelves, with small spaces in between that a lot of people would struggle to squeeze through. Nothing is labelled or in any order that I can understand, just stuff crammed in wherever it fits. There's fake food, musty old books, cauldrons and potion bottles, and metal goblets that look like they're meant for drinking your victims' blood.

In the far corner there's a life-size scarecrow straight out of a horror movie, with a sack and straw face, its neck bent at an unnatural angle. I take a few steps towards it, trying to see the details in its face through the shadows and dust.

Its eyes are matte-black holes, gaping wide, staring out at me.

'Boo!' a voice shouts from right behind me, making my insides lurch like I've been dropped off a cliff. I spin around fast and stumble backwards into the scarecrow, which starts to lean and wobble. For one moment all I can see is its face leering over me, the stained checked shirt full of maggot holes crushing down on top of me like, it wants to absorb me into its body. Then it stops. Lifts slightly.

'Give me a hand, Angelo, this dude is heavy as freak.' Gus's blond head appears next to mine, and together we push the scarecrow back up to standing. 'Well, that went better than I expected,' Gus says, looking annoyingly pleased with himself.

'Jesus!' I'm trying to get my breathing back under control, so it's all I can manage. 'What the hell?'

'You didn't hear me coming, did you? I was like a stealth-master – nay, a stealth-god. I was a freaking golden jackal. Yessss!' He punches the air.

'What about our rule?' I say. 'No flinching each other.'

'But we're not in a round, so I wasn't flinching you – I was just practising.'

My heartbeat has dropped to a less explosive speed. I've stopped feeling like I'm going to puke. My internal organs feel more or less where they should be. And Gus looks so proud. Like my little brother when he beats me at something.

'You are a golden jackal,' I say. 'You properly got me.'

'I did, didn't I?' Gus grins. 'Although this big guy helped a bit.' He nods at the scarecrow. 'He looks a bit like my uncle Mikolaj. I wonder if I can use him in the game?'

'You don't need him,' I say. 'You bossed that. I had no idea you were there.'

'Next round of Flinch, I am in it to win it,' Gus says.

And at that moment our apps sing out for the

start of a round. *Half a pound of tuppenny rice
. . .* Gus's face lights up.

'We're playing then?' I ask.

'Obviously.' Gus grins. 'This pile of junk can
wait.'

'Just one thing,' I say, as we back out of the
cupboard and prepare for battle. 'If you really
want to strike fear into your opponents' hearts,
you might want to go for something a little more
ferocious than "boo".'

'Don't knock the classics, Angelo. A trillion
flinching babies can't be wrong.'

I pause at the steps back up to the corridor.
There's always a burst of noise and activity as
the Flinch app plays, as people take up their
positions and get ready for action. As soon as
the music stops, there's silence. A silence full of
unknowns. Every player waiting, watching,
noiselessly buzzing. We're ready.

CHAPTER SIX

THE RETURN OF UNCLE MIK

'Where are we heading?' Gus whispers. 'Is there anyone else even on this floor?'

'There's someone here,' I say. 'I heard them when I came up. Let's go find them.'

In the dark passageway, lit only by the neon gashes across the walls, everything looks distorted. The door to our right is a step closer than I thought it was, and I have to pull myself back from smashing into it face first. The glass panel in the door that lets you see through to the other side has been painted black, so our only visibility beyond comes from the slim crack of light at the bottom. I crouch. Gus crouches behind me. I watch the line of yellow, waiting for a flicker of movement.

'Is it clear?' Gus whispers. 'I'm getting a cramp.'

I count another fifteen seconds, resisting the urge to cough, or scratch my itch, or do anything that might give our position away, and nod. 'I think so, let's move.' I push the door open a few centimetres, have a quick look, then open it wide enough for me and Gus to walk through. I blink a few times because the light is much brighter here. We're in another rehearsal room – this one with floor-to-ceiling mirrors covering the left and right walls. It's full of chairs, most of them pushed to the edges of the room, some of them strewn across the wooden floor.

'There's nowhere to hide in here,' I say.

Gus shakes his head and points at a stack of

chairs in the corner, half hidden behind one of the black curtains that can be pulled across to cover the mirrors. 'Over there,' he whispers.

The space behind the curtain and chairs doesn't look human-sized to me – there's no way someone is hiding there. 'It would have to be someone the size of a two-year-old,' I say.

'Nah, they could be one of those circus people who can bend their bones and fold up their bodies to fit into tiny spaces.'

'Do you think you might have noticed if there was someone like that at school?' I ask, but I'm moving towards the curtain anyway, so we can check it out to put Gus's mind at ease.

'We should poke it with a stick,' Gus whispers. 'If only I had Miss Pointy with me – she'd know what to do.'

'You mean Miss Pointy as in the stick that you used to fight the spiders?' I risk a glance at him. 'You kept her?'

'Of course I kept her, she saved my life,' Gus says. 'Sticks deserve gratitude too, Angelo.

She's living happily in stick retirement in my wardrobe.'

'I'm just going to do it,' I say. And I rush forward, leaping over the chair obstacle course, and yank the curtain back at the same time the room falls into total darkness.

It takes me a moment to work out what's happened, but over Gus's panicked breathing, I hear the sound of the door closing. I can't see if there was someone behind the curtain, but I'm ninety per cent sure that Gus and I aren't alone in the room any more.

'Angelo,' Gus says, his voice coming out in a squeak.

'Don't move,' I say. 'Listen. Whoever's in here with us . . .' I try to make my words sound firm and unafraid, 'is as blind as we are. If they do anything, we'll hear them.'

I close my eyes and try to calm myself so I can listen, putting one hand on my chest in an attempt to steady my heart, my other hand sliding to my pocket for my phone. The bees inside are wild again, and I'm literally itching to move.

There's a faint creak somewhere behind me. I don't flinch, just focus. I'm good at this game, and I don't like losing points. My fingers feel the reassuring smoothness of my phone, and I wrap them around it, pulling it out of my pocket as quietly as I can.

There's a breath somewhere behind me to the left, close enough that I feel the warmth of it. I hold my thumb over what I hope is the right place on my phone screen to turn the torch on. Resist the urge to take a deep breath. Nothing announces that you're about to make a move like taking a big gulp of air.

A moment before I press, a light from somewhere else rips through the darkness. The sudden brightness sears my eyes, so I'm just as blind as I was in the pitch-black. I instinctively blink, and when I open my eyes, it's to get just a second of a glimpse of my own wild face reflected in the mirror, and the huge figure of someone looming behind me. Then there's a thud, and the light goes out.

Gus swears. I take a leap forward, away from whoever is behind me, and hit the torch on my phone, spinning around to shine it into their eyes. Their vacant black eyes in a sack-cloth face.

'Uncle Mikolaj,' Gus says from somewhere on the floor. 'Why would you play us like this? We're family.'

It's the goddamn scarecrow.

I shove it away, angry that it scared me so much. It crashes down on to a couple of chairs, so loud that anyone who wasn't already stalking us will be after us now.

I swing my torchlight around and see Gus crouching down to pick up his phone.

'Was that your torch the first time?' I say.

'Yeah.' He's checking his screen to see if it's cracked.

I don't want to blame him, but I'm annoyed. 'Can't believe you dropped it.'

Gus looks up at me, and even in the bad light, I see something like hurt on his face for a moment. It makes me feel like a snake.

'Sorry, man, it's not your fault,' I say.

'I didn't drop it, though,' Gus says. 'Someone knocked it out of my hand.'

It crosses my mind that he's making this up to cover his mistake. Would he lie? I've not known him for that long.

'Are you sure?' I say. 'That's against the rules.'

Gus frowns. 'Yeah, I'm sure, Angelo. You think I'd make it up?'

I shake my head, mad at myself for even considering it. 'Nah, course not. This game is making me hella paranoid.' I step over a chair and offer him a hand up. He hesitates, then takes it, and gives me a grin.

'Dude, it's a head-wrecker,' he says. 'The question is . . .' and he turns to the scarecrow, 'who are you working with, Uncle Mik?'

'And where are they now?' I say.

I shine the light down on to the scarecrow.

It took both me and Gus to set it back straight when it fell on me in the prop room. It's heavy. Whoever got it in here that fast must be strong. I think about the masked figures in the woods.

'Gus,' I say. 'You know the people Nai and I saw yesterday in the Dread Wood?'

'You think they're back for another round?'

'The big one could have moved the scare—'

'Please address him by his proper name,' Gus interrupts me.

I sigh. 'Uncle Mikolaj. I don't think anyone in Year 7 could, and there are only Year 7 kids here. Everyone else has gone home.'

'What about Shaheed?' Gus says. 'That guy is one buff boy.'

'Even Shaheed,' I say. 'And anyway, didn't he get one of the main parts? He'll be in the hall belting out a power ballad or something.'

'He has the voice of an angel.' Gus nods. 'So maybe the smug sixth-former snuck back just to mess with you.'

'Maybe,' I say. I don't think so. 'Let's get out

of here and see if we can salvage anything from this round.'

'I'll get the lights,' Gus says, heading back to the door we came in through. I shine the torch so he can make his way through the chairs without tripping and watch him flick the switches on the panel. Nothing happens. He flips the switches again, and again, but the lights stay off. 'Someone has really got it in for us,' he says.

I hear something behind me – the door at the other end of the room whispering shut. I whirl around, cursing myself for taking my eye off the ball. Gus walks into a chair behind me, I think – I hear the crack of bone on metal, but I keep the torch arcing across the other end of the room.

'Little help?' Gus says.

'Hang on a sec,' I say. 'Just one minute.'

'What is it?'

I don't answer, just scan the area around me, trying desperately to locate the threat. And in the wobble of the torchlight that makes the room look tilted and full of shadows, I finally spot it. In the corner Gus made me check, behind the stack of chairs. I'd pulled the curtain away the moment before the lights went out. Now it's swinging slightly, and there's a bulk to it that wasn't there before.

There's someone there.

CHAPTER SEVEN

BEHIND THE CURTAIN

'Gus,' I say, pointing at whatever it is that's waiting for us underneath the heavy black drape.

'Maybe Uncle Mik brought Auntie Agnes,' Gus whispers.

'Stand behind me with your torch and keep an eye on that door,' I say, as quietly as I can. 'I don't want anyone else sneaking up on us.'

Gus nods and picks his way through the chair graveyard towards me, turning on the torch on his phone and keeping it focused on the other end of the room to the thing behind the curtain. I decide not to count down in case whoever is after us uses that time to pull another move. Instead I dart forward and yank the cloth hard and to the left, sending it swinging across the pole.

I don't expect the loudness of the scrape of metal on metal as the drape moves, and the sound makes me grit my teeth. What I see in the murky space behind the curtain makes my heart jolt.

'That's definitely not Auntie Agnes,' Gus says.

It's a mannequin, like the kind you see in clothes shops. It's wearing a weird mix of old-fashioned clothes – a long, ruffled dress, a waistcoat that looks like it belongs to a Victorian chimney sweep, and a red feather scarf. The worst part is . . .

'Is that the mask your creeps were wearing yesterday?' Gus says.

'Yeah,' I say, glaring at the painted rubber skin, the bloody curve of the lips, and the dagger teeth. The head of the mannequin sways slightly, and the wisps of yellow hair float like feathers on the breeze.

'I can see why that would freak you out,' Gus says. 'Not me, obviously, I'm a pro-level flincher, but Smiler here could definitely scare a lesser player.'

We stare at it for a few seconds, the dark looming around us, even with the light from our torches. I'm suddenly desperate to get out, somewhere light, under the actual sky and with air that doesn't feel choked with dust and sweat.

'Let's move,' I say. 'I want out of the drama rooms.'

'This is still just a game, right?' Gus asks.

I rub my eyes. They feel full of grit. 'I'm not sure any more,' I say.

'Where next?' Gus asks.

My mind is flicking through the options when something strikes me. 'I didn't see this stuff in the prop cupboard. Where did it come from?'

'Looks like it's all from the costume stores – they had a few mannequins in there when I was collecting something last week.'

'The costume stores . . .' I say.

Me and Gus look at each other. 'Hallie,' we say at the same time.

We both turn and run, jumping chairs and thumping through the door, back into the glow-in-the-dark corridor, through the black rehearsal room and out of the drama department. Then we're on the stairs, running down as fast as we can without stacking it, and heading towards the last place we saw Hallie.

The building is so quiet. We don't see anyone as we run, but to be fair, we don't stop to look. There are so many hiding places in here – pillars, art displays, dark corners. I can't shake the feeling that we're being watched. There's an itch at the back of my neck, and I'm sweating – it's like my whole body is screaming a warning to my brain. It doesn't feel like a game. It feels like danger.

I haven't been in this part of the block before, so Gus leads the way to the costume stores.

'Through here,' he gasps, as he flings open a side door into another one of those godawful mini corridors. It's the same as the prop stores, I realise. Two steps down, and then a low door that you'd never bother noticing. But this door is closed and has a chair wedged under the handle, keeping it that way.

Then we hear a familiar voice bellowing from behind it. 'Whoever's doing this, you're messing with the wrong person. I'm going to tear you apart when I get out of here,' followed by a stream of sweary insults.

'Hallie,' I call. 'We're going to let you out.'

I don't think she hears me. She's moved on to describing the creative ways she's going to savage the person who shut her in.

Gus winces. 'I'll let you go first. I already have an extra hole in my body for my stoma. I don't want Hallie creating any more.'

I pull the chair, but it's angled in tight and it

barely moves. I wiggle and slide to the sound of Hallie's rage, and eventually feel it budge. I wrench it out and throw it aside, and go to pull the door handle down, but she gets there first. The door flies open, and I fall into the storeroom on top of Hallie, who kicks out at me – still not realising I'm a friend.

'Hal, it's me,' I say, trying to defend myself from the torrent of punches to my head.

'Angelo?' Her voice sounds muffled underneath me. She stops pummelling.

'Yeah,' I say, trying to untangle myself from her and the floor and a load of costume junk that's fallen on top of us.

'Oh, sorry.' She's out of breath and red-cheeked. 'Someone–'

'Shut you in,' I finish, reaching out a hand to pull her up. 'You know who?'

'No idea,' she says. 'But I will find out, and when I do . . .'

'You're going to peel their face off with your fingernails,' Gus says. 'Among other things.'

'Gus, you're here too.' Hallie looks up at him at the top of the steps. 'Yay.'

'Nice to see you, Hal.' Gus grins. 'Tell me, is it really possible to do those things with a pirate boot that you described?'

'It was all I had to hand.' She waves a boot at him. Then her mouth falls open and her eyes widen in shock.

I turn to see what she's seeing.

Two masked figures are standing behind Gus, gloved hands reaching towards him. There's a shove and a shout, and Gus falls into the stores, sending all of us crashing over again. The last thing I see before the door slams shut is that jagged plastic smile, and I know that whoever is under the mask is smiling in just the same way.

Gus is up first and trying the door, but it's jammed shut again.

Hallie hurls herself at it, because trying the same thing that doesn't work over and over again seems to be her default reaction when she's storming. But then, I figure, maybe two of us could do it. So I join her, flinging myself at the door with everything I have. There's not much room, so we hit each other as often as we hit the door, but we don't stop until we mess up our timing and collide head-on. I stagger back into a rack of costumes and drop to the ground, the wind knocked out of me. Hallie backs away, holding her forehead and growling with pain.

Then someone speaks from the other side of the door.

'There, there, sweetlings, you rest now. There's nothing to be gained by fleeing a sealed fate, and you know we always win at games.'

I'm frozen on the outside, while inside my mind is recoiling like it did the time I accidentally walked in on my mum in the bath. I don't want to believe what I've just heard. But . . .

'That was her. That was Mrs Latchitt,' Hallie gasps. 'Wasn't it?'

'Literally no one else in the world talks like that,' Gus says. 'We're screwed.'

'Wait,' I say. 'They might still be out there.'

I put my ear to the door but hear nothing. I sit on the floor and lower my head to peer at the crack at the bottom of the door. There's maybe two centimetres of light seeping through, but it's weak. Barely light at all. Hard to tell if there's anything moving out there.

I rest my cheek on the floor and stare into the glow. Think maybe I see a flicker, then nothing. I edge forward, just a little, the scummy smell of the carpet filling my nostrils, bits of dirt and trodden-in gum squishing into my skin. Nothing moves.

'I think they've go—' I say, just as something shoots through the gap under the door and straight towards my face.

CHAPTER EIGHT

UNDER ATTACK

I yell out and push myself off the floor as fast and hard as I can, smashing into the same costume rack again, sending it scudding into another rack that topples on to some shelves which come crashing down, sending everything flying. In the cramped, echoey room, the noise is like an explosion, ricocheting off the walls and filling my head. The air is full of dust and debris – dead-skin flakes and bits of hair from students who left long ago. It floats all around us, and the thought of breathing it in makes me want to puke.

'Made you flinch,' Mrs Latchitt's voice giggles from behind the door. I hear them walk away – two sets of footsteps, and a creepy whistling of the Flinch tune – as the chaos settles around us.

'What the hell was that?' Hallie is looking around frantically. There's junk everywhere – hats, wigs, smashed glasses, broken shelves – and somewhere in the middle, there's . . .

'It was a snake, right?' Gus has backed up against one of the walls. 'It looked like a weird snake.'

'I don't know,' I say. I was almost too close to see. I just got the blur of an outline as it rushed towards my eye. 'Maybe.'

'Where is it?' Hallie pushes a pile of costumes with the toe of her shoe.

'I'd rather not find out,' Gus says. 'If it belongs to the Latchitts, it can't be friendly.'

I scan the room, searching for movement.

'Whatever it was, it was small,' I say. 'Maybe ten centimetres long, right?'

Gus and Hal nod.

'So we'll be able to handle it when we find it. I mean it's not going to be stronger than us.'

Something darts out from under a heap of junk, skims across the floor and under another pile before we can even move.

'But it's faster than freak,' Gus says.

We move closer together, keeping our eyes on the place we last saw it.

'You think it's poisonous?' Hallie whispers. 'It's got to be, right?'

We know the Latchitts like to modify their creatures before they send them out into the world. I nod. 'Seems likely. We need to catch it to be sure.'

Gus groans. 'You say catch it, I say squish it.'

'Either way, we can't let it get out of this room and disappear into the school,' I say.

There's another flash of movement, over by the back wall. Hallie charges forward, kicking and shoving stuff out of her way to get to it. 'Where is it?' she shouts.

'Over there.' Gus points at an as yet unbroken set of shelves against the wall. 'I saw something white behind those boxes.'

We make our way through the rubble to the shelves. There's no sound apart from our breathing, and no movement. We stand perfectly still, watching, trying not to blink. And then a strip of white flies from the shelves at head height, straight at Hallie's face.

She screams and instinctively puts her arms up to protect herself. It hits her wrist and takes a deflection, veering off back towards the corner by the door.

We turn to see it disappear under the costume racks.

'Dude, it flies,' Gus shouts.

'That's not like any snake I've ever seen,' I say. 'Did you see its body? It was segmented.'

'It flies.' Gus is pale and sweating.

'And never mind its weird-ass body,' Hallie

squeaks. 'It has freaking teeth.'

'And,' Gus says, 'did you guys notice that *it flies?* It's a flying toothy snake.'

I pick up what looks like a shepherd's crook from the floor and empty out a box of what I think (hope) are fake beards. 'We need to corner it,' I say. I spot another smudge of white as it zips across the room. I leap and slam the box down, missing it by an embarrassing amount.

'Let me try,' Hallie says. She puts on the pirate boots – 'To protect my legs,' – and grabs a bucket. Then she tears into the last place we saw it, tossing stuff aside and stomping on fallen urchin trousers and lacy dresses in her too-big boots. 'Where is it?' she growls.

'Look out!' Gus shouts suddenly, and I see it just after he does. The creature drops from the ceiling on to the back of Hallie's head, latching on to her hair with its teeth.

Hallie freezes for a second. Her face is turned away from us. 'It's on me, isn't it?'

'Don't panic,' I say.

'But yes,' Gus adds.

It starts pulling itself up her braid, and Hallie freaks out, spinning round and round, twisting her neck to try to see where it is. 'Get it off me!'

We both rush towards her, and I try to grab it. But it's so fast, and for a thing with no apparent eyes or ears, it seems to know exactly which direction I'm coming from. Hal is screaming and can't keep still, and I just miss it as it shoots out from under my fingertips. I make contact once only, and my hand comes away with smears of slime where I touched its skin.

I hear Gus rummaging behind me. 'When I whistle, Hallie, go totally still, and Angelo, take a step back,' he says.

'Got it,' I say. I hope he knows what he's doing. 'Hal?'

'Do it,' she says. 'But make sure you get it.'

Gus whistles. I jump backwards, and Hallie stops moving which must be so hard when every instinct is willing her to keep fighting.

Gus is swift. He uses a piece of broken wood to flick the creature off the back of Hallie's head, hard enough to send it flying smack into the wall. It drops down on to the ground, then slithers away again.

'Oh god, thank you,' Hallie says, looking at Gus like she might kiss him.

'Don't look so surprised,' Gus says. 'I do have some skillz, you know.'

One of the piles of junk at our feet shifts slightly.

'Where is it now?' I say, turning circles like a confused noob.

'This is like being in the trash compactor in *Star Wars episode four*,' Gus says, circling too. 'It could be anywhere under this lot and we're never going to be one step ahead of it.'

Hallie picks up another shelf and starts using it to sweep aside the junk on the floor. 'We need to clear a space,' she says. 'Where it can't hide and we can see it coming.'

She's right. Gus and I start sweeping too, and

I'm annoyed at myself for not thinking of this. It's like I've totally lost my head, and that's not something I usually do.

'Anyone have eyes on it?' Hallie asks, out of breath. We're all hot, coated with grime and sweat.

'Negative,' Gus says.

'It will come to us,' I say. 'It's a hunter like the spiders.'

So we stand in the space we've cleared, eyes on all corners of the room, and we wait.

It takes longer than expected for it to make its move. Regrouping maybe, after its collision with the wall. It soars at us out of the darkest corner of the room, but it's not as fast and we have the space and time to see it coming. I delay until the last possible moment, then lift the beard box, hoping it will fly inside and I can slam it down and contain it. But it veers away.

Hallie's ready with what looks like a nun's robe – a large black cape of heavy cloth. She throws it over the creature and the whole lot thumps to the floor. Then Hallie is on it in her pirate boots, screaming and jumping and stomping, like she took the attack on her head really, really personally.

'Hal, wait,' I say. But she's lost in her fury. She doesn't stop until our phones sing out. *Pop goes the weasel.*

We all jump.

'I forgot we were playing,' Gus says.

I push my hair back off my face. I'm so done. 'Yeah. Didn't feel like playing.'

'Do you think it's dead?' Hallie is staring down at the fabric under her feet.

Me and Gus look down too.

'Reckon so,' Gus says.

Hallie steps off the cloth and I use the shepherd's crook to lift it. Slowly, carefully. Just in case.

Underneath, ground into the floor, is a mush of white goo, bits of it stuck to the cloth and peeling away like bubble gum. There's not enough solid matter left to even scrape into a test tube.

'I think it's dead,' Gus says. 'And man, it stinks.'

We stare at the mess formerly known as 'unidentified creature', and I wonder what the others are thinking. There's a tangle of thoughts and questions in my mind, and I can't decide which one to pull out first.

A rattle at the door makes me jump – again – and we all turn to face it. I have no energy left to run, or to fight, and I can't make my body ready up for action. Gus looks the same. Hallie less so – she's on the alert again, and is lifting the bucket, ready to launch it at whoever's outside. But Hallie has reserves of rage as deep as the Marianas Trench when something she cares about is on the line, and she definitely does not want another snake flying at her head.

'Hallie, are you in there?' a voice calls out, as the door handle jiggles.

Hallie lowers the bucket. 'Colette, thank freak it's you. Get us out of here, will you?'

There's another rattle and a bump, and the

handle lowers and the door opens. Colette is standing in the doorway, her shirtsleeves rolled up and her hands flecked with paint. She already looks confused, and that's before she notices me and Gus, and the carnage behind the three of us. Her mouth drops open. 'What the actual . . .?'

'We were attacked,' Hallie says, at the same time that I say, 'Something happened,' and Gus says, 'Dude – snakes can fly.'

Hallie tries again. 'Colette, we were attacked.'

Colette stares at us. 'By flying snakes?'

'Just the one,' Gus says. 'But that was enough. And it had teeth like this . . .' He makes his mouth into a circle shape and uses his fingertips to be the teeth, holding them up to his face like fangs.

'It wasn't exactly a snake,' I said. 'I mean, it definitely had physical elements that were more like a worm.'

'A flying snake-worm?' Colette says.

'With teeth like this.' Gus does the thing

again.

Hallie puts her hand to the back of her head. 'It bit my hair.'

Colette raises an eyebrow. 'Your hair?'

'Why did it bite her hair?' Gus asks. 'Because now that we've said it out loud, that does seem, you know, weird.'

'I'm not sure it was aiming for her hair,' I say. 'That was just where it latched on. It looked like it was trying to move around to her face.'

'Shut up,' Hallie shrieks. 'You never said!' And she's panicking again, rubbing herself all over to make sure there's nothing on her.

I shrug. 'Didn't think it would help at the time.'

'But what did it want with Hal's face?' Gus says. 'No offence, Hal, but if I was a flying, toothy snake-worm, Hallie's face wouldn't be somewhere I'd want to park myself.'

'That is offensive, Gustav. But you notice that it went for my face and not yours, so it obviously has good taste.'

'Nah,' Gus says. ''Cos it didn't have any eyes. If it had eyes, it would have been all over me like my second cousin Julia at a family wedding.'

A huge snigger blasts out of me, so violently that a bit of snot shoots out of my nose and flies through the air. Hallie and Gus erupt too, and then we're all laughing. So hard. I crouch down, arms around my stomach, feeling the already tired muscles pull and ache.

Hallie's face is scrunched in on itself, tears trickling down her cheeks, and she drops to the floor next to me. She's not even making any noise now, just silently shaking with laughter. Gus joins us on his hands and knees, thumping the ground with his fist, making a weird squeaking noise as he laughs. This goes on for a few minutes before we can pull it together.

'What the actual hell?' Colette says. 'I have literally no idea what's going on.'

'I mean we don't really, either,' says Hallie, rubbing her face and somehow managing to make it look even more dirty.

Gus looks up at Colette. 'But we do know one thing: your nana and grandpops were here.'

CHAPTER NINE

THEY'RE BACK

'm going to text Naira,' I say. 'See if she can get over here – we all need to be around for this.' I tap out a quick message on my phone.

'You mean the Latchitts are in the building?' Colette says.

'You just missed them.' Gus is slowly pulling himself off the floor.

I look up from my phone. 'Nai's on her way.'

Colette has turned white and looks like she might pass out. I jump up the steps to where she's standing and sit down, patting the ground next to her for her to join me. 'They were here, but I'm sure they've gone now.' I put my arm around her shoulder and give her a squeeze.

'Yeah.' Hallie's rebraiding her hair. 'Round's over.'

'What?' Colette says.

'We'll explain, I promise,' I say. 'Soon as Naira gets here.'

Hallie looks at the devastation in the room around her. 'And we need to try to clean this up fast, or I'm going to be in another Saturday detention, and the last thing I need is a Back On Track session right now.'

'With added Latchitt,' Gus says.

She nods. 'Yeah. Being chased by psychos on a weekend morning is pretty much as bad as life gets.' She looks up at Colette. 'No offence.'

'Sometimes my mum makes me go to car boot sales on weekend mornings,' Gus says. 'That's pretty grim too.'

Colette is picking at a splodge of dried paint

on her wrist. Imagine your life being messed up so much by people you've never even met. And imagine if they were family. Her mind must be racing. We can't hide this from her though, not now we know for sure.

I hear the thud of feet on wooden floor, and the hallway door flies open. Naira skids to a stop when she sees Colette and me. 'Where are the others?'

'Hey, Nai,' Gus calls out. 'We're in the cupboard of terror.'

She peers over mine and Colette's shoulders into the costume stores. Takes it all in. 'They're back, right?' she says.

'Yeah,' I say, standing up and feeling at least half the muscles in my body strain and twitch. 'They are.'

She looks at each of us and rolls her eyes. 'You're all wrecked and we need to sort this out. I'll take charge.'

We're too done to argue, so we listen as she tells us all what to do, and then we get on with our tasks, even though it hurts.

'Did you not get flinched, Naira?' I ask, because she doesn't look like she's been playing.

'No, no one in the hall got the notification,' she says, stacking up pieces of broken wood from the shelves. 'Would have been hard with the teachers around anyway. Must have just been you guys.'

I'm picking up anything that looks like a fake beard or moustache and putting it back in the box. Weird that it was just us who got alerted when there was a much bigger group of players in the hall. Almost like it wasn't random. Like someone planned it that way.

Is it possible that the Latchitts are controlling Flinch?

'So talk,' Naira says. 'Tell me exactly what happened.'

We replay the story as we work, starting with me and Gus in the prop room, and ending with Colette finding us.

Naira asks loads of questions, but Colette doesn't say anything, just keeps her head down

111

and carries on putting costumes back on hangers.

'Right,' Naira says when we've finished. 'At least now we know for sure.'

'Do we, though?' Colette says. 'I mean, is it definitely them? You didn't see their faces.'

'I'll never forget her voice.' Hallie shudders.

'And let's look at our Latchitt bingo cards,' Gus says. 'Uses olde words and phrases that no normal people say, like "fleeing a sealed fate".' He holds up a finger. 'Giggles at things that frankly aren't at all funny . . .' Another finger.

'Calls us sweetlings,' I say. We all make a face.

'She said they always win at games too,' Hallie says. 'Like she did when we were on the science block roof.'

'And the freaky whistling, of course,' Gus says. He's holding up eight fingers now, which doesn't seem right but I get his point.

Naira nods. 'One of them is huge, and the other is tiny.'

'And let's not forget the fact that they are targeting us – AGAIN – because they hate us,' Hallie says.

'And using modified versions of creatures to attack us,' I say.

We've all stopped what we're doing and are looking at Colette.

Gus holds up ten fingers. 'Bingo.'

Colette takes a breath, straightens up. 'Well, when you put it like that, it could be anyone.'

The others all open their mouths to argue, but I've been a victim of Colette's sarcasm too many times, so I wait.

She smiles. 'Relax, doofs, I believe you. The Latchitts have come back, and they've brought a new creation. My first thought is that I'm really freaking sorry for accidentally bringing them into your lives, forcing you to face life-or-death situations and have biting worms in your hair. My second thought is more of a question, really . . . why are they back? And what are we going to do about it?'

'That's actually *two* questions, Colette,' Gus sighs. 'Maybe they came back to teach you your numbers 'cos they didn't get to do it when you were two.'

'What were you doing when all this was going on, Colette?' Naira says. 'You only came down after they'd gone, right?' She asks casually, but I see her side-eying Colette.

'I was playing Flinch up in the art rooms. There were about ten of us up there, so it was quite . . .' she hesitates, looking for the right word, 'fun, I guess. I came looking for the others once the round finished. I didn't know anyone was in danger from a mutated snake-worm, otherwise I would have come sooner and brought my collection of shurikens.'

'What are the chances they only had one of the snake-worms?' Gus says. 'Because if so, that problem has been fully smushed.' He points at the nun cloak still on the floor. The bits of creature are drying and crusting up now, like white scabs.

'Like, no chance,' Hallie says. 'They want a family, remember? I bet they've made loads of those ugly critters.'

'We need to think of a better name for them,' Gus says. 'Snake-worms is lame – it'll never catch on.'

'I agree,' I say. My mind is spinning. 'They'll have more of them. And what if the Latchitts are the ones behind Flinch?'

'What, and they're using Flinch to sneak into school and attack us?' Naira says, looking horrified. Then she nods. 'It's perfect – everyone's separated, nobody knows where anyone else is, and they can get away with wearing the masks in case anyone does see them.'

'Snworms,' Gus continues, randomly. 'No, that sucks.'

'Nobody knows where Flinch came from in the first place, right?' Colette says. 'I mean, who started it, or when exactly? It just appeared out of nowhere.'

'But why?' Naira says. 'Why come back and go to all the trouble of creating Flinch? They could find much easier ways of getting to us.'

'They like games,' Colette says.

'And creepy old nursery rhymes.' Hallie straightens a stack of boxes.

'Nai's got a point, though,' I say. 'The Flinch app is slick – it must have cost some bucks to develop. Where are they getting their money and resources from?'

Naira tries and fails not to look smug that I said she had a good point. 'I doubt their jobs at Dread Wood High would have paid that much, and they don't even have those any more. Do you know if they were rich back when your mum was still with them, Colette?'

'I don't think so,' Col says. 'I mean, my mum hasn't said much, but from what she has told me I'd say they weren't rich or poor, just normal.' She snorts. 'Well, normal in money terms.'

I slide a stack of cowboy hats across one of

the remaining shelves. 'And they're genetic scientists, not app developers . . .' I think back to our confrontation with them in the clearing, when it sounded like there was a third person hiding nearby. '. . . Is it possible that someone else is helping them?'

We all pause what we're doing as we let that thought turn over in our minds. The Latchitts are terrifying. The idea of the Latchitts with money, resources and potentially someone helping them is terrifying times one hundred.

'I don't know if it helps to think that way,' Hallie says. 'They're not questions we can answer right now and we'll only do our heads in worrying about it.'

'Yeah, let's focus on the things we can do something about,' Gus says. 'Come on, guys, good names for flying snakes. Let's put our heads together.' He goes back to sweeping broken glass into a pile in the corner.

I think about the creature, trying to get a clear image of it in my mind. It was so fast and everything was so chaotic that I never got a really good look at it. The way it moved . . . 'I'm not so sure it actually flew,' I say.

'Tell that to the back of my head,' Hallie snorts.

'I mean, it was more like it propelled itself into the air – like a boosted jump. I didn't see any wings.'

'Spitting straight facts, man,' Gus says. 'No wings, just wormy, muscly segments, attached in a line. And teeth at one end, like this.' He does the thing with his mouth and fingers again.

Naira pushes a rack of costumes against a wall. 'But it moved like a snake across the ground?'

'Yeah,' I nod. 'Fast. Powerful.'

'Like you wouldn't believe,' Hallie adds.

'Maybe the name should be more focused on the teeth aspect,' Gus says.

I rub my hands, remembering the feeling of it on my skin. 'And it was coated in some kind of mucus.'

'By mucus you mean slime?' Colette says.

'Freaking perfect.' Hallie puts her hand up to her hair. 'I'm never going to be able to wash that out.'

'You know what it looked like?' Gus says. 'Have you ever seen a butcher making sausages? They take these empty white skins and then pump them full of meat so they're fat and juicy.'

'Gross,' Hallie says.

'Delicious,' Gus says. 'Anyway, my mum used to make me go to the butcher all the time, and I used to hate looking at the piles of skins all white and shiny, coiled up in trays on the bench. Mr Snake-Worm looked like that – an unfilled sausage skin, waiting to become plump with succulent innards.'

'Why are you wearing pirate boots, by the way, Hallie?' Naira stops, puts her hands on her hips.

Hallie rolls her eyes. 'For smushing, obviously.'

'Hair-biter!' Gus says. 'No, that sucks too.'

'I've been thinking about what you said, Gus.'

I roll my shoulders and wince when they crack.

'The thing about cousin Julia?' He looks at me. ''Cos that was said in the heat of the moment and must never leave this room.'

'Well, that,' I snort. 'But also the bit where you asked what you'd do if you were a flying snake.'

'Are we questioning the snake's motivation?' Colette says. 'Wasn't it just to attack?'

I must have watched thousands of wildlife documentaries and though every species is different, there are some behavioural patterns that are standard in the natural world. 'Seems too simple,' I say. 'It had no reason to attack us seeing as we weren't in its territory and we didn't pose a threat.'

'You think it wanted to eat Hallie?' Naira says.

'I don't see how it could. It was too small to consume a human.'

We put the last of the rubbish in a pile by the door and look around at the tidied-up stores.

'It's not too bad,' Naira says. 'You can

probably get away with saying you tripped on a rack which knocked into the shelves and broke them.'

'Thanks for your help, Nai,' Hallie says. 'We were wrecked.'

'I have an answer for you, Angelo,' Gus says. 'If I were a flying snake in a new territory, the first thing I'd want to do is find myself a nice, cosy nest.'

'A nest,' I say, and I let that sit in my mind to see how it feels. Makes sense. 'I wish I knew exactly what it was, or at least what creatures it has in its DNA. It'd be much easier to get some answers.'

Colette sighs. 'I hate this. Because of me you're dealing with masked weirdos and unknown hostile monsters that either want to eat you or build a nest in you.'

'It'll be all right, Col,' Hallie says, putting an arm around her. 'At least they're smushable little freaks – that gives us more of a chance against them than we did against the spiders, and we blew those suckers to pieces.'

'And that was also my fault,' Colette says. 'You must wish you'd never met me.'

I want to tell her that meeting her was one of the best things that ever happened to me. That fighting spiders with Hallie, Gus and Naira changed my life in so many amazing ways. That I wouldn't change any of it. But I can't say that. So I go with, 'None of this is your fault, Col. We were in detention that day because of the things we did. It was right that we faced the consequences.'

'Yeah, we totally deserved to go in the Latchitts' burn book,' Hallie says.

'But you didn't deserve to be hunted by killer spiders,' Colette says.

'Kind of feel like I did a bit,' I say.

'Naira definitely did,' Gus says. 'Total scumbag. And have you heard her singing? Death by spider is the least she deserves.'

Naira whacks him in the arm. 'Hey!'

And we all crack up laughing.

'Seriously, Col,' I say, when I can speak again. 'You're not responsible for the Latchitts' actions.'

'I just want to punch them really hard,' Colette sniffs. 'Wearing gloves so I don't have to touch their evil, wrinkly skin.'

'We all do,' Hallie says. 'And we will. You'll see.'

'Yeah,' Gus says. 'We've got this.'

I want to agree. I do. But worry bites at my brain and itches at my neck. If we had this much trouble with just one of the worms, how would we fight off a whole pack of them?

One thing I'm certain about, though. Whatever the Latchitts are planning this time, we'd be fools to underestimate them.

CHAPTER TEN

THE ARRIVAL

I plan to stay up googling types of worms and snakes to see if I can put anything together, but by the time I get home I'm exhausted. I don't ever remember being this tired. I manage dinner with Mum and Raph, and a couple of games with him before his bedtime, and then I'm asleep on the sofa until Mum sends me off to bed with a kiss and a hair ruffle. I like her being at home in the evenings.

In the morning, I still feel like I've been through twenty rounds with a heavyweight.

We all agreed to meet before school so we can try to work out what the hell is going on, but it's too early, and I could have used the extra twenty minutes in bed.

'Looking fresh, Angelo,' Naira says, when I meet her at the entrance to our estate. I'm annoyed to see that she looks as perfect as usual. Clean uniform, no creases, shiny hair. I look like I slept in my clothes. Yesterday's round of Flinch has a lot to answer for.

'Morning,' I say with a nod.

'So what's the plan?' Naira asks. 'Did you come up with any genius insights overnight?'

I shake my head. 'I'm going to figure it out today, though – what the worm is. There's something I remember seeing or thinking when we were in the Latchitts' lab back in November, but I can't place it.'

'Not to put the pressure on,' Naira shoots me a look, 'but you need to try harder.'

'Yeah, no shiz, Nai,' I say. 'Did you come up with anything useful? Because I don't see why it's all on me.'

'It's on you because you're the one who knows this stuff,' she snaps. 'Some of us spend our evenings doing homework instead of watching pointless TV shows.'

'Not pointless though, are they? If you're relying on me to be a wildlife expert.'

She snorts, and I feel myself getting properly angry.

'Something to say, Naira?' I ask.

'Just that for a wildlife expert, you're pretty clueless about what we're dealing with here,' she says. 'You have one job in the group. One job.'

That stings. 'Because I've never seen anything like it in any documentary, ever. I know about snakes – there are thousands of species across the world – and this isn't any of them. So I'm thinking it must be a worm–'

'Snakes or worms, what does it matter?' Naira says. 'They're basically the same thing.'

'They are not even slightly the same thing!'

I roar, unable to keep a lid on my anger any more. 'They're completely different. And it matters because knowing or not knowing what we're dealing with could mean life or death.'

'So quit spending your time daydreaming about Colette, and put the effort into finding out,' Naira shouts. 'Do the work, man. One job!'

'It's a shame algebra and war poetry's not going to help us protect ourselves from the Latchitts, isn't it?' I'm still shouting, and I hate it. ''Cos that's the only way you'd be any help in this situation. This is why you never had any proper friends, Naira – you're smug, boring and no fun to be with. I was much happier when I didn't have to talk to you every day.'

'Fine,' Naira says. 'Go back to your trash-fire of a life and stay away from me.' She storms off ahead, and I turn to go back home.

I've walked maybe five or six steps before I regret what I said. Six months ago, I would have carried on walking, but things have changed. So I stop, turn and jog to catch up with Naira. We're friends, and everything we've been through means something.

'Naira,' I call. 'Wait up.'

I expect her to ignore me, but she stops straight away like she was already thinking about it.

'I'm sorry,' I say. It's still hard, but I've got better at apologising lately. 'My head's trashed and I'm tired. I shouldn't have said those things. I didn't mean them.'

'Me too,' she says. 'I feel angry all the time at the moment, and it doesn't take much to set me off. I didn't mean what I said about the trash-fire.'

I'm more relieved than I would have expected to be. It doesn't sit comfortably, but I remind myself that I can trust Naira. I can trust all my mates. I need to hold on to that. We walk towards school again.

'We need to keep it together,' I say. 'The Latchitts would love seeing us raging at each other.'

'Yeah, they would.'

Naira glances around, and I know that she's wondering the same thing as me – are the Latchitts watching us right now?

It's early enough to feel cold and alien out on the quiet roads we use as a shortcut to school. I wish I'd worn my hoodie, and I wish there were more signs of normal human life around us. I could really do with the comforting wheeze of a bin lorry loading up, or the rattle of letters being delivered by the postie. We walk faster.

'Let's try to work out the snake-worm paradox together,' Naira says.

'Get you with the big words,' I say.

'It means–'

'I actually know what it means.' I *think* I know what it means, and that's good enough for me. I'll blag it.

'Sorry,' Naira says.

'It's OK.'

'So what makes you think it can't be a snake?'

'The physiology,' I say, trying not to feel too

smug about wheeling out a big word of my own. 'No eyes. No visible tongue. All snakes have tongues – they rely on them to make sense of their surroundings. It's how they smell.'

'OK,' Naira says. 'But the thing that attacked you yesterday had teeth, right?'

I nod. 'Right.'

'I didn't think worms had teeth.' She shudders.

'Usually they don't,' I say. 'But there's a couple of worm species that live underwater that do, I think.'

'So that's a good place to start researching,' Naira says. 'Maybe the Latchitts used some DNA from those.'

'Yeah,' I say. 'Maybe. It's a start. Thanks, Nai.'

'Forget what I said before. We're in this together,' she says.

We finally turn on to the main road, and the first thing we see is a fleet of trucks, trailers and caravans rolling along and turning into Finches Green. The funfair.

'They've arrived,' I say. 'Gus will be buzzing.'

We wait at the entrance to the green for a gap between trucks, watching them manoeuvre through the tight space, like they've done it a million times. The biggest ones – those carrying a flat-packed Ferris wheel, dodgems and what looks like a tower of death – take a while longer to make the turn. Traffic backs up, and I can hear car horns beeping and angry shouts further down the road. The rides look strange on the trucks – brightly coloured scaffold bars and huge slices of sidings covered in badly painted murals.

'It all looks so flimsy,' Naira says. 'Are we not worried about going on dangerous equipment that only takes two days to put together? It's just bits of wood and a few screws.'

'But it comes every year,' I say. 'And nothing bad has ever happened – we would have heard about it.'

'Nothing bad has happened *yet*,' Naira says.

One of the drivers, hauling a caravan, slows and waves us across, so we do a half walk, half jog on to the green. Instead of cutting straight through the middle like usual, we skirt the edge. The grass is still morning wet, and the 6 a.m. mist that blankets the green hasn't lifted yet. It looks like something out of a ghost story, which wouldn't usually bother me, but, like I said, I'm jumpy. We walk fast.

A honking horn right behind us makes me lurch forward, tripping on the uneven ground, and almost falling right on my face. I just about manage to steady myself and turn to see the biggest truck so far, churning through the mud towards us, its headlights carving through the mist and lighting up all the tiny specks of moisture in the air. We move out of its way, and watch as it parks up at the edge of the green where the parkland meets the churchyard.

'Of course there's a ghost train,' Naira says, eyes fixed on the side of the trailer. 'Where's the last place you'd want to play a round of Flinch?'

There's a sea of classic monsters and horror

movie villains painted across the truck. Skeletons, zombies, chainsaw-wielding murderers. All slightly misshapen and deformed – cross-eyed faces, body parts out of proportion, six-fingered hands, and legs bent at unnatural angles. They're like cheap tattoos. In the centre of it all, leering over the swirly 'Ghost Train' lettering is an old-fashioned jack-in-the-box, popped open to reveal a killer clown with a mouth full of dagger teeth on a coiled spring.

'Yeah, that's got to rate pretty highly on the most stressful Flinch locations chart,' I say. 'Alongside city morgue at night, and zombie-infested tower block.'

Naira makes a face. 'Insect house at the zoo. My actual worst nightmare.'

'Take any of those places and add the Latchitts,' I say. 'Now that would be the *actual* actual worst.'

We exchange looks and turn our backs on the ghost train, hurrying towards school, our friends, and hopefully a Flinch-free morning.

CHAPTER ELEVEN

PARASITE

It's here, it's here!' Gus skips over to us when we reach the school gate. 'Did you see?'

'You mean the creepy, death-trap fair?' Naira says. 'Yeah, we saw it.'

'Isn't it beautiful?' Gus sighs.

Hallie's looking at her phone but manages to roll her eyes. 'Glad you two are here – he's been unbearable.'

I hear a car pulling up behind us, and turn to see Colette getting out. She smiles like she's happy to see us, but she looks tired and worried. I can't imagine what it's like for her, having crazies like that for grandparents and knowing they're somewhere nearby, watching and waiting.

'Dude, your mum is super young,' Gus says, smiling and waving at Mrs Huxley a bit too much. 'Does she have a boyfriend?'

Hallie punches him in the shoulder. 'Gustav, do not be shipping yourself with Colette's mum. That's disgusting.'

'Not shipping,' Gus says, rubbing the spot where Hallie hit him. 'But out of interest, Colette, tell me more about her . . . What does she do? For work . . .' He side-eyes Hallie and moves himself so he's out of reach of her punches. 'And for fun?'

'She's an assassin,' Colette says. 'Black belt in eight different martial arts and flies a chopper like a bad-ass.'

'Really?' Gus gasps.

'Obviously not.' Col rolls her eyes. 'She's a PA

to some director in a software security company. She schedules Zoom meetings and organises stuff.'

'Hmm, organising,' Gus says, nodding like it's his favourite thing.

'Careful, Gus,' I say. 'Cousin Julia will get jealous.'

'How much did you tell your mum about what's going on?' Naira asks, once Col's mum has left.

'Nothing,' she says. 'She'll freak out and keep me off school, won't let me out of her sight. And we'll be fine at school if we stick together, right? What can my grandparents really do to us here?'

'Lock us in a cupboard and chuck a snake at us,' Hallie says, as we start walking up the drive.

'Speaking of . . .' Gus pulls a folded piece of paper out of his pocket. 'I have come up with the best list of potential snake names. Something to please everyone. Guaranteed you're going to love them . . .' He coughs to clear his throat.

'Actually, we've established that it isn't a snake,' says Naira.

'What?'

'It can't be a snake,' Naira says. 'No tongue.'

'Well, that's just peachy.' Gus rips up the paper and stuffs it back in his pocket. Colette gives him a comforting pat on the arm.

'So if it wasn't a snake . . .?' Colette says.

'A worm,' I say. 'Which I don't know as much about.'

'Let's see if the library's open,' Colette says. 'We can google on one of the computers while we talk. It should be really quiet in there right now.'

'Because all the normal people are still getting up and eating breakfast?' I ask.

'Yeah, but all the cool kids are here.' Colette smiles. She hands me a chocolate bar and I grin a thank you at her.

Hallie is still scrolling through her phone as she walks. 'Hold up, Mum has an update on Michelle.'

None of us say anything, just watch as she reads her message, checking her expression to try to work out if it's good or bad news.

'Eww,' she says.

'What?' Gus is trying to read over her shoulder.

Hallie puts a hand up to tell him to stop and carries on reading. All is quiet apart from the crunch of gravel under our feet, and the distant chug of trucks on the green.

'Eww,' she says again.

We're almost at the mansion now – the oldest part of the school. I take the lead, heading towards the side door that I know is most likely to be unlocked. Dread Wood High is as quiet as I've ever seen it – just a few cars in the car park, a couple of squirrels in the trees, and no other signs of life.

The battered door creaks as I pull it open. That's one of the things about the mansion part of the school that catches people out. From a distance it looks so fancy, like something from a movie, pillars and stained glass, and ceilings decorated with gold plaster roses. But when you look close up, you notice that everything has seen much better days. It's all scratched and chipped, with bits flaking off, and strange-coloured patches where things have been badly repaired. Everything creaks.

'So,' Hallie says finally, as we're walking up the stairs to the library. 'The vet found something on Michelle's scan. Something awful.'

'Are you going to tell us what?' Naira sighs. She has a low tolerance for Hallie's drama-queen behaviour early in the mornings.

'Well . . .' Hallie takes a deep breath and squeaks open the library door. The library is dark inside, but the lights flick on, one by one, as we walk in. The large room is cold and quiet, and has the feeling of being empty of people, though there could be someone behind any of the bookcases. We walk over to the computers and stand around Hallie while we wait for her announcement.

'It's some kind of . . .' she pauses again, 'parasite.'

'Eww,' Gus, Naira and Colette say at the same time. But my mind is racing.

'What kind of parasite?' I ask. 'Do you know?'

Hallie rolls her eyes at me. 'I didn't exactly ask for details. There's a parasite inside my chicken, Angelo. It's disgusting and awful, and deeply distressing.'

'And it might be a worm,' I say. I dump my bag on the floor, wheel back one of the computer chairs and wiggle the mouse until the monitor whirrs to life. I'm trying to stay calm so I can log in without my hands shaking, but I feel like I've just hit on something. My brain is fizzing.

'What is it, Angelo?' Naira says.

'When we were in the basement, trying to find Hallie,' I say, tapping in my password, 'we walked past a load of doors which we didn't have time to look behind. Some of them had signs up – Latin names of creatures I assumed the Latchitts were using in their experiments.' The system is logging me on, painfully slowly. 'There was one that I think was . . . I just need to check. I'll know it if I see it.' I open a search window and type in 'parasitic worms'.

I feel the others all gathered behind me. Hallie is messaging furiously on her phone. My eyes scan the pages, quickly reviewing and clicking through to the next. I'll know what I'm looking for when I see it.

'Tapeworm,' Hallie says, just as I find the right page.

'Tapeworm.' I point at the screen. 'Also known as cestoda. The Latchitts had them in their lab.'

We all stare at the search page, and I'm sure the others are feeling as grossed out as I am. They're not beautiful creatures.

'That is freaking ugly,' Gus says.

'Is one of those in Michelle?' Hallie sits in the chair next to me.

'Well, it doesn't look exactly like what we saw in the costume stores,' I say. 'But the Latchitts probably messed with it. Hal, is there any chance you can get them to show you the scan? Just so we can be sure?'

'I'll try,' she says, tapping at her phone again.

'Michelle used to belong to them, right?' Colette says. 'To the Latchitts?'

'Right,' Naira says. 'They looked after all the school chickens.'

There's a silence where I'm sure the others are remembering what happened to the rest of the chickens on the field. Death by mutant spider.

'So they were using them in their experiments then?' Colette asks. 'They deliberately put a parasite inside Michelle?'

'Of course they were,' Gus sighs. 'Why did we think this was over?'

'Hang on, I'm just calling Mum,' Hallie says, shoving the chair out from underneath her and stomping off a few metres.

Colette takes the chair and sits. 'The worm that attacked you yesterday . . . You thought it was trying to bite you, but is it possible that it was trying to get . . .' She stops talking. Makes a face.

'Get what?' Gus asks.

But I know what she means.

'The slime,' I say. 'Could be some sort of lubricant.'

Naira starts gagging.

'What?' Gus says again. 'What are you talking about?'

'I'm just saying that if it's a parasite, it would be looking for a host,' Colette says.

'A host?' Gus looks from Colette, to Naira, to Hallie – who is arguing with her mum on the phone – to me.

'A living host,' I say. 'A parasite needs a live body to grow inside.'

'Oh my god,' Gus says. 'Oh. My. God.'

'I think he's got it,' Colette says.

Gus pulls out another chair and sinks down on to it. 'So I was right when I said it would be looking for a nice, cosy nest,' he says. 'It wants a human nest. We're the nest, guys. We. Are. The. Nest.'

'She's sending the link that the vet sent her,'

Hallie says, leaning over my shoulder and grabbing the mouse. 'It's a video, apparently. She didn't want me to see it because she thought I wouldn't be able to handle it. I told her that was an infringement of my rights as Michelle's owner.'

'Are we ready for this?' Colette says.

'It has to be done.' Naira moves closer to the screen. 'We need to know for sure.'

'Here.' Hallie clicks.

We all peer at the monitor. It takes a few seconds for me to get my bearings within the 3D image. The camera is moving across Michelle's body as she lies on her side, obviously fully sedated. My eyes move to the stomach area, looking for the worm.

'I can't see it,' I say. 'You guys?'

'I literally have no idea what I'm looking at or for,' Gus says.

'The worm should be inside the stomach, which I think is right here.' I point at the screen. Everyone leans in.

'It should be in the stomach because . . .?' Gus says.

'Tapeworms live in the intestinal tract so they can feed off whatever the host eats,' I say. 'They grow bigger and bigger, while the host loses weight.'

'Is it that blobby thing there?' Colette points.

'I don't think so,' I say.

'Ugh, there's something moving right there.' Gus stabs at the screen.

'That's her heart beating,' Naira says.

We stare at the moving image, edging closer and closer. We must be missing something.

'Maybe it's really tiny,' Colette says. 'I mean, how big a worm could fit inside a chicken?'

Then I spot it – movement where there shouldn't be any. But it's not in the digestive system.

'There.' I touch the screen where I see it – a slow, almost gentle writhing, at the lower end of Michelle's back, near her tail. The camera zooms in on it. They've spotted it too.

We watch in silence. I don't think any of us are breathing.

I see a long, segmented body, shifting and kneading, like it's massaging inside Michelle's body. But it's not inside her stomach, it's wrapped around her spine. As our view moves upwards towards her neck, I can see that it's much longer than the worm from the stores – maybe five times as long, curled around and around the delicate bone.

It's when we reach the end that things get really sick.

'What in the holy scrut is happening there?' Gus gasps.

Hallie starts gagging, and I don't blame her.

The face of the worm is just like the one we met. No eyes, no ears, just a round gaping mouth, filled with hooked needle teeth. The worm inside Michelle is using those teeth to anchor it, by biting into . . .

'. . . the brain,' Naira whispers. 'It's biting the base of the brain.'

'Is it a freaking zombie worm?' Gus says. 'It eats brains instead of food?'

Hallie runs out of the library, slamming through the side door. I hear her footsteps clattering up the empty corridor.

'I don't think it's eating the brain,' I say, already turning to go after Hallie. 'I think it's using it for something else. I'll get her.'

I run the same way Hallie did, wanting to reassure her that her chicken isn't about to turn into the living dead. It's only when I'm halfway down the corridor deeper into the mansion that I remember we'd agreed to all stay together.

And that's when the Flinch app starts singing.

CHAPTER TWELVE

BENEATH THE DOOR

I swear out loud, but I don't stop running. The others are together. Hallie is alone. I need to get to her. If the Latchitts are here, and I'm certain they are, somewhere, they're going to want to pick us off one at a time. They'll hunt Hal down first. I need to find her before the tune runs out.

I hear footsteps on the lower floor, right under where I'm running, so I head for the back stairwell, ignoring the 'Sixth-Formers Only' sign. The stairs are wooden and winding, and hella loud at every step, but they're the quickest way down. I leap them, two to three at a time, praying I don't trip and stack it. I think there are girls' toilets on the corridor below, and judging by how much Hallie was trying not to puke, I reckon that's where she's heading.

That's the way the money goes . . . The music stops as I hit the lower floor, echoing slightly in the dim old corridor. And then there's nothing.

I look left and right, trying to remember where the girls' toilets are. I've never really paid attention, for obvious reasons. I hear a drip from down the hall to my right, and jog that way as quietly as I can, feeling thankful for broken taps.

The door to the girls' toilets is half open. I hesitate outside for a second or two. I've never held back from going into places I'm not supposed to. In fact, I generally see it as a challenge that makes me even more determined to get in. I've been everywhere in Dread Wood

High. Except . . . this is the girls' toilets.

I look up and down the corridor. I can't see or hear anyone. So I take a deep breath and nudge the door with my knuckles, just hard enough to open it to a width I can squeeze through. Then I step inside.

The first thing I notice is the smell. The room smells grim, even this early in the morning when it's at its cleanest. There's a tang of bleach in the air, but the undertone is the same as every public toilet: old urine and god knows what else, mixed together in that specific way that lets you know it will never, ever go away. No matter how hard the cleaners scrub. But – and this really annoys me – it's not half as strong as it is in the boys' toilets.

The sink area is to my right: four stained basins sunk into a counter underneath four cracked mirrors. The taps on two of them are dripping. The ceilings are high, and the walls stark, so the sound bounces around the room. There are exposed pipes everywhere, running up the walls and across the ceiling in parallel lines, then mazing off into different gaps and holes in the brickwork. They gurgle, randomly, and make me feel like I'm in the pump room of a junked-up spaceship in a creepy sci-fi movie. There are small windows, set high in the walls, the frosted glass distorting the light coming in from outside. Each has four square panes of glass, separated with a cross, like the windows my little brother puts on every drawing of a house he ever makes, even though hardly any windows are actually like that. The floor is grey, the walls dirty white, and when I walk further into the room and turn right again, I see the toilet cubicles are dark blue. There are ten – two rows of five opposite each other. Some of the doors are wide open. Three of them are closed.

I turn into the space between the rows of cubicles, trying not to let my shoes squeak on the tiles. My instinct is to run away, as fast as I can. I mean, of course it is – I am in the girls' toilets and it feels all kinds of wrong. I don't call out, just in case, but I need to know if Hallie is behind one of those doors.

Same as the boys' toilets, the doors don't go all the way from the floor to the ceiling – there's a gap, of maybe twenty-five centimetres at the bottom, a little less at the top. Wide enough to peep through. Although I find myself wishing I hadn't thought of the word 'peep' because that has added massively to the wrongness.

The first door on the right is shut and has a handwritten 'OUT OF ORDER' sign taped to it. Someone's drawn faces inside the 'O's. I put my ear to the door and hear nothing but dripping. I crouch down and tilt my head. All I can see is the base of the toilet. The next locked door is the second on the left, so I stay low and turn to look under it. As my face lowers, my cheek almost pressing on the ground, I hear the main door to the toilets creak open. I freeze, my eyes still facing the gap under the cubicle door, and I listen. There's a soft footstep behind me.

Someone's coming into the room.

I have just a few seconds before they'll turn towards the cubicles and see me. It could be one of the others – Hallie even. I still don't know if she's in one of the locked toilets. She's not in this one, anyway. Through the gap under the door, all I see is the dull shine of white ceramic toilet base. I feel a moment of relief. But then I blink, and something slides into a view. A foot lowers from somewhere above the gap where I can't see. It's enormous – a well-worn dark boot with a thick, ridged tread, about twice the length of my school shoe. The second foot joins it, easing down carefully, firmly, to rest on the floor beside the other. I swear my heart stops for a second, along with the hearts of every one of those bees inside my body.

Mr Latchitt is in the cubicle.

I have no time. With someone behind, and I have a horrible feeling about who that might be, and Mr Latchitt just centimetres away, there aren't many options open to me. I spring off the ground and dart into another toilet cubicle, using the noise of Latchitt opening his door to close mine. I step back from the locked door, leaning against the toilet-roll holder and wondering how the hell I'm going to get out of this. Apparently my heart has started beating again, because it's thumping so hard that it feels like it could make the whole room shake.

Then the whistling starts. *Pop goes the weasel*. That weird-ass nursery rhyme that I used to be so excited to hear blasting out of my phone. What were we thinking back then, at the start of Flinch? We should have known there was more to it. It was never just a game.

Two sets of footsteps tread slowly across the tiles like they have all the time in the world. I hear a sniff and some movement in the cubicle to my left, which was the third locked door that I hadn't had a chance to look under yet. I duck down and peer under the wall to see Hallie's feet. At least I think they're her feet – I don't spend much time looking at people's shoes. She must know the Latchitts are in here. She must be losing her mind. I wonder what her plan is, if she has one.

My phone vibrates in my pocket, so I pull it out and have time for the quickest glance at the message in our group chat: *6f toilets, Ls r here* – I mean, it's Hallie, of course her plan involves her phone – and then the whistling and the footsteps stop.

There are one, two, three seconds of silence, and then the cubicle walls and doors start rattling, as someone shakes them from the outside.

'Rat-a-tat-tat, come out, little piggy,' Mrs Latchitt giggles.

Hallie screams.

'I'm coming, Hal,' I shout, and flatten myself to the floor, gritting my teeth at the crunch of my jaw on the tiles, and the thought of all the scum that must be on them. There's just enough room to fit my head under the wall, and I look up to see Hallie's shocked face as my disembodied one slides into her cubicle.

'Oh my, there are two little piggies here,' Mrs Latchitt squeals. 'Such merriment! Come hither, little piggies.'

'Give me a hand,' I gasp at Hallie, and she snaps out of her surprise, backs up against the wall and reaches for my arms to help pull me through. It's not easy. There's hardly any space and I have to bend my body into painful angles, but I finally get my head and shoulders through. Hallie's cubicle door judders in the frame, so hard that it hurts my head. Hallie's eyes are wild, but she gets a firm grip on my wrists and pulls hard.

I'm finally slipping across the tiles, into Hallie's cubicle, when I'm suddenly jerked backwards by a yank on my leg. Someone's grabbed my ankle. My body skids much faster backwards than it did coming in, until my chin smashes into the bottom of the cubicle wall. My teeth clash together and I taste blood in my mouth. There's a streak of pain through my chin that's as bad as anything I've ever felt in my life. Hallie screams again. But she doesn't let go.

It takes me a moment to get myself together. I'm dazed, and I can't remember what I was supposed to be doing. I feel pressure on my ankle and on my wrists, and I'm being pulled in both directions so roughly that I feel like I might snap. Then Hallie shouts down at me. 'Kick, Angelo. Kick!'

And I kick.

CHAPTER THIRTEEN

BIG BAD WOLF

It's amazing how much strength you can find when you need to. I kick once, twice, but the grip on my ankle doesn't loosen. I feel the skin being scraped off my shin as my leg is pulled through – must be into the unlocked cubicle on the other side of the one I hid in. Which means there's another wall between me and my attacker. I scrabble with my loose leg, try to get some purchase on the floor, but it's slippery. I know if I can bend my knee high enough and get a foot on the inside of the wall, the leverage will be enough to propel me back towards Hallie. So I put everything I have into an upwards kick with my trapped leg. It cracks painfully against the bottom edge of the wall, but whichever Latchitt is holding me wasn't expecting it. The hold releases, just for a second, and I use that time to pull back, slam my foot against the wall, and push. I shoot backwards, crashing into Hallie's cubicle.

'Our piggy is a sly fox,' Mrs Latchitt says. 'Let us snare him.'

I pull myself into a sitting position, and slump against the toilet, wheezing and shaking. Hallie crouches down, half next to me and half on top of me because there's barely room for both of us. 'What do we do?' she whispers.

'We hold out in here for as long as we can,' I say. 'The others got your message too, right? They'll find a way to help.'

'I think you'll find your bunny friends are tucked up tight in their burrow,' Mrs Latchitt says. 'Nobody's coming for you.'

I look up to see the lock on the cubicle door start to turn.

'Grab it!' I shout, jumping off the floor and ramming my hand down on the metal bar that keeps the door shut. It slams down, but then starts rising again under my palm.

Hallie moves to help, but there's only space for one of us on the lock, and her crushing my hand even harder into the metal isn't going to do me any favours. 'Shout for help,' I gasp. 'Try to open a window.' Because this has gone way beyond trying to do this on our own.

I hear Hallie climb on to the toilet seat. 'I can't reach,' she says. 'It's too high. We need to swap.'

I'm taller than Hal, but not by much. I look up at the window to see if there's a chance I'll be able to get to it, and then a masked face appears in the gap at the top of the cubicle wall from the one I hid in.

'Peekaboo!' The gaping eyes are tilted to the side, the mouth grinning, the neon hair dancing like candy floss on the air. And then a gloved hand appears, and it's holding something.

'Hallie, look out!' I yell.

She looks up and screams as the worm dangles over her head. It's about the same size as the one from the stores, the length of its body like a line of connected segments. Each section is just a couple of centimetres long, and then it pinches in, like a waist, before the next one starts. It's white, and it glistens with slime. It's being held from the tail end, so the face is pointing down towards Hallie. No eyes, or ears, or any other features that I can see, just a circular mouth full of teeth. It's twisting and jerking around, the mouth opening and closing, like it's desperate to launch itself away from the hand gripping it.

'Close your mouth,' I say. 'Cover your ears. That's where it will try to get in.' It's all I can do to help. If I let go of this lock, we're history. The metal is pushing into my hand relentlessly, but I keep pushing back.

'Clever foxy,' says the voice of Mrs Latchitt, and it comes from the masked person holding the worm. 'You are a wily one.'

Hallie pulls her blazer over her head and clamps her mouth shut.

'Your nose,' I shout, and she wraps the blazer so it covers most of her face. She should be safer, but it means her hands aren't free to do anything else.

My hand, chin and leg are throbbing. I'm sure I'm bleeding from multiple places. I can't protect my own bodily openings, and I can't even begin to put a number on how much I don't want that worm crawling inside me. I start to panic.

Hallie is screaming inside her blazer and trying to get as far away from Mrs Latchitt as she can.

We can't do this. We can't escape. We can't fight. Game over.

A noise blasts out around us. Loud and urgent. The pressure under my hand stops. The masked face above us visibly jumps. It's the fire alarm, and the Latchitts weren't expecting it.

Hallie slips off the toilet seat, whacking her head against the wall, at the same time that Mrs Latchitt drops the worm and disappears from the gap above us. I take the risk of letting go of the door lock to fling open the toilet seat. The worm drops into it and I smash the lid down again. The entrance door to the toilets creaks and I hear footsteps moving away from us, down the corridor.

We sit there for a few seconds, trying to catch our breath. At some point the Flinch app sounds for the end of the round, but I barely hear it. The scream of the fire alarm doesn't stop.

'We've got to get outside before someone finds us here,' I say, dragging myself off the floor.

Hal is leaning on the toilet seat like a wrestler pinning someone down for the count, and I don't think she wants to let go.

'Any movement?' I ask, nodding at the toilet.

'No, but we can't just leave it there. We have to check.'

I nod. 'Open the lid on three?'

'OK,' she says. 'On three.'

I take off my blazer and hold it up, ready to net the worm if it jumps out. 'One . . . two . . . three.'

Hallie lifts the toilet lid and jumps back while I move over the bowl with my blazer. There's nothing inside the toilet. Except the usual stains and grimness.

'It's gone,' I say. 'I hope they can't swim . . .' I don't finish the sentence. If it can swim and survive in water, then we've just unleashed a dangerous parasite into the water supply. We could have started something that might infect the whole town.

I'm pulled out of my spiralling doom thoughts by Hallie yanking on the toilet flush like her life depends on it.

'Just in case,' she says.

Then we pick ourselves up, try to brush off the worst of the pain and the blood, and make our way outside. Walking casually is difficult when every step hurts like a raging beast, but I do my best to stroll outside with my usual lack of concern for authority.

There's a group of people standing around on the gravel at the front of the mansion, including Colette, Gus and Naira, who are talking to Mr Canton. They try to hide their relief when they see us walking towards them, but I see it. They were scared. They know something went down.

'What the jeepers happened to you two?' Mr Canton turns towards us and looks us up and down. 'You need medical attention.'

'Nah, we're good,' I say.

'Yeah,' Hallie says, and I see a purple lump swelling above her left eye. 'All Gucci here.'

'Angelo is bleeding, and you have a nasty bump, Hallie. Have you ever been inside a Gucci outlet store? It's sparkly and intimidating, and they'd never let you two in looking like you've just been in a pub brawl.'

Mr Canton has moved in for a better look at my cut chin. 'Right,' he shouts above the alarm, which is switched off at that moment. Everyone in the grounds turns to look at him, including all the kids who are streaming up the drive to school wondering what's going on. It's almost time for registration. 'Right,' he says again, in his normal voice. 'You five, come with me, please. Inside, now.'

CHAPTER FOURTEEN

THE PRIMROSE ROOM

There's no point arguing, so we follow him back into the building. We exchange looks, and I'm desperate to know what happened to the others, but there's no chance to say anything with Mr Canton on the alert. He's tapping away on his phone.

'Gustav, Naira and Colette, you are physically unharmed, correct?' Mr C says. They nod. 'So you three sit yourselves down in student services and I'll be back to speak to you in a few

167

minutes. Miss Heeps is coming to sit with you.' He looks up as Miss Heeps walks through the door with her travel coffee. 'Ah, here she is. Thank you, Miss Heeps. Apologies for interrupting your breakfast.'

'It's fine,' Miss Heeps says, but her face says different.

'Hallie and Angelo, we're going to meet Mrs Parekh at the Primrose Room.'

Hallie and I both groan, and Gus gasps.

'Please not the Primrose Room,' I say.

'Kids that go there are never seen again,' Gus whispers. 'Or else they come back . . .' he looks around at all of us, 'different.'

'Mr Gustav, I'm glad to see that your unique imagination hasn't been impacted by the stressful situation you've found yourself in this morning,' Mr Canton says. 'But there is absolutely nothing wrong with the Primrose Room.'

'If you're a serial killer, an evil hypnotist or a cannibal nurse,' Gus says.

'Mrs Parekh is not a cannibal,' says Mr C.

'But you're not ruling out serial killer?' Gus says.

I can't help myself – I let out a snort of laughter. It really hurts.

'You three, in there with Miss Heeps.' Mr Canton holds the door open for them. 'Angelo and Hallie, with me. No arguments.'

Colette and Naira follow Miss Heeps into student services, and Mr Canton starts leading us up the corridor to the Primrose Room.

'Nice knowing you, guys,' Gus calls after us. I turn and grin at him.

Mrs Parekh is waiting for us at the bottom of the small flight of stairs to the Primrose Room. It's one of the only places in school that I've never been, because, like the girls' toilets, I've never wanted to. Kids who are sick generally go straight home. Only kids who are *really* sick, either physically or mentally, come to the Primrose Room. Sometimes it's used for counselling. And Gus is right, some of the kids who come here end up leaving school, or being off for weeks. I don't think Mrs Parekh is eating them, though. She shakes her head when she sees us.

'Isn't it a little early to be getting yourselves in this kind of state? I've unlocked the room. In you go.' She points us up the six steps and stays to talk to Mr Canton for a minute while we creak into the room.

It's bigger than I thought – not as big as a classroom, but bigger than a usual office. It's separated into different areas which all look equally like places I don't want to be. There's a bit with a bed, soft chairs, inspirational quotes on the walls and pictures of dolphins and sunsets. There's a part with just a couple of chairs facing each other, with a small table to the side with a box of tissues on it. There's an area with a sink, shiny countertops and boxes of medical equipment. I'm betting the cupboards contain bowls for vomiting in. Hallie and I stand in the middle of it all, breathing in the smell of bleach and flowers and sick people, and I suddenly just want to go home.

'Now . . .' Mrs Parekh comes quickly into the room. 'Hallie and Angelo, is it? Let's see what we're dealing with.' She points to some chairs by the shiny area. 'Sit.' We sit. She opens some doors, comes back with a cold pack and a first-aid kit. 'Hold this to that potato coming up on your head,' she says to Hallie, who puts the cold pack on her bump. The she pulls up a chair uncomfortably close to mine and comes at me with the antiseptic wipes.

It takes about twenty minutes for us to convince Mrs Parekh that we're fine. Hallie doesn't show signs of concussion, and my chin and mouth have stopped bleeding, so she finally agrees not to call an ambulance. I don't show her my hand or my leg, which are both stinging like a beast. The thing is, I don't feel fine. And I don't just mean the pain. I feel totally done in – like I'm being sucked into a black hole of sadness and exhaustion. I roll my eyes at myself for being dramatic, but at the same time I feel the truth of it. I have never felt this low before. This drained, and tired, and worried. A massive part of me wants to be tucked under a blanket by some kind paramedic and sped away to hospital where I'll be safe from the Latchitts, and I can just sleep.

It's actually Hallie that keeps me going. She's sore and coming down from the shock of what happened in the toilets, but she's doing it much better than I am. She's chatting to Mrs Parekh, covering for me, trying to carry me along with her while I struggle to act normal. It's weird. A role reversal.

'Fine,' Mrs Parekh says, finally. 'I will tell Mr Canton that you can join your friends in student services, but you must sit quietly and drink some sweet tea. I'll be coming to check on you in half an hour, and you must let me or Mr Canton know if you feel faint, or have a headache, or become unwell in any way. Understood?'

We nod. Hallie stands. 'Come on, Angelo.' She nudges me, because I'm still sitting.

'You're sure you're all right?' Mrs Parekh frowns at me.

I'm not, but I know I have to be. We need to stick together, and we need to talk so we can work out what the hell we're going to do about the Latchitts. I can't leave the others to deal with this without me.

'Yeah, I'm good,' I say, pulling myself out of the chair, just as we hear a knock on the door.

'Everyone decent?' Mr Canton's voice calls into the room.

'Oh god,' Hallie says. 'Why would he say that?'

'Come in, Mr Canton,' Mrs Parekh says. 'They're ready to go.'

Mr C opens the door and bounces into the room. 'Ah, looking much better,' he says.

'We all know that's not true.' I wince as I talk because my lip is swelling up.

'Are you OK to call their parents, Mrs Parekh?' Mr C asks.

'No, do not call my mum,' Hallie says. 'I mean it.'

Mr Canton looks surprised. 'You know we have to, Hallie. You've sustained an injury at school, and we have to follow proper safeguarding procedures.'

'But she's got enough to deal with today.' Hallie's voice is getting louder. 'And I'm fine, so I really don't think it's necessary.'

Mrs Parekh looks concerned. 'Is there something going on at home? I noticed that nasty half-healed scratch on your cheek.'

'Oh god, that's nothing,' Hallie says. 'Tell her, Angelo.'

'Her chicken has a parasite,' I say, trying to back her up.

'Come again?' says Mr Canton.

'Her chicken has a parasite.'

Mr Canton blows out a breath and shakes his head. 'You know, I thought I knew all the current lingo you kids use, but this one must have passed me by. Is this a new slang phrase for something?'

'No,' Hallie says through gritted teeth. 'My chicken literally has a parasite.'

'Ah, but literally doesn't mean literally any more, does it?' Mr Canton says. 'Sorry, guys, you're going to have to spell this one out for me. And there I was, thinking I was poggers.'

I can't help it, I start laughing. Hard enough to hurt, which maybe isn't saying much because everything is roaring with pain. Hard enough to make me feel less hopeless. After a second, Hallie laughs too.

'Mr C, I have a pet chicken. She's at the vet's. She has a parasite, which is making her act crazy, which is how I got the scratch on my face.'

'Oh, right,' Mr Canton says. 'You meant *literally* literally.' His face lights up. 'Excellent news – that means I am, as I thought, still poggers.'

Hal and I laugh again, and she stops arguing about them calling her mum. Mr Canton leads us back to student services, where the others are waiting.

'You're alive!' Gus whoops, as we walk in the door.

'Thank you for your assistance, Miss Heeps,' Mr Canton says. 'I'll take over from here if you have something to get back to.'

Miss Heeps rushes off like she's just been given a second chance at life.

'Hot choccies for everyone?' Mr Canton says, walking to the vending machine.

'Only if you stop calling it hot choccie,' Naira says, but she's smiling.

Colette pats the seat next to her. 'You OK?' she says, as I carefully sit myself down.

I make a face that I think best sums up how I'm feeling. 'Are you?'

She looks pale and tired, but like she's hanging on better than me. 'I am,' she says. 'Surprisingly, since we've been stuck in here with Miss Heeps. Your face might hurt but I feel like I've had my soul sucked out. Glad you two are here now.'

Mr Canton brings over a tray of hot chocolates and hands them out.

'Ooh, there's an extra one,' Gus says when there's a cup left on the tray. 'Can I have it?'

'This is for me, Gus,' Mr Canton says, settling into one of the seats. 'You've already had one. You're not the only ones who've had a stressful morning.' He takes a sip. 'Besides, we need to talk, and none of us are leaving this room until I find out exactly what's been going on.'

We all look at each other. We haven't planned for this. None of us know what to say.

'Something's been happening in school over the past few weeks,' Mr Canton says. 'Something that involves at least half the pupils at Dread Wood High. And I suspect you five know what it is.'

Despite how scrutty I'm feeling, I instantly jump into high-alert mode. I see the others do it too – shifting in their seats, pressing their lips together, paying attention. With everything that's happened, Flinch has become a nightmare. But if we snitch, and the rest of school finds out about it, our lives at Dread Wood High won't be worth living anyway. Either way, we're screwed.

CHAPTER FIFTEEN

AN ALLY

'Let's start with an easy question,' Mr Canton says. 'Why were you in school so early today?'

'We just wanted to hang out,' Hallie says. 'We didn't get a chance to yesterday, because of the performance stuff.'

'Ah yes, we'll come back to that in a moment,' says Mr C. 'Why did you go up to the library?'

'Because of Hal's chicken,' I say. 'Hallie got a message from her mum that the vet had found a parasite. We wanted to look it up on the computer so we could understand what's going on.'

'We don't really know much about chicken parasites,' Colette says. 'It's never come up before.'

Mr Canton nods. 'Same, actually. So you were in the library, researching chicken parasites, and then Hallie and Angelo left the room . . .' He turns to Gus to continue.

'Hallie was upset,' Gus says. 'Because we saw some images of the parasite, and it looked like a sausage skin with teeth.'

'You felt sick, didn't you, Hal?' Naira says.

Hallie nods. 'So I ran out to the nearest toilets, thinking I was going to vom everywhere . . .'

'. . . and Angelo followed to make sure she was OK.' Naira starts retying her ponytail, even though it's perfect.

'But there must have been a wet patch on the floor in the toilets,' Hallie says. 'Because I slipped when I was running in and smashed my head by the sinks.'

'Got it,' Mr Canton says. 'And how did you end up with your injuries, Angelo?'

'I heard Hallie yell out, and the thud when she hit her head,' I say, and I already know that there's no way to make this last part believable. 'So I ran into the toilets, and . . . slipped too.'

'In the same wet patch?' Mr Canton raises an eyebrow.

'The taps in there are broken,' I say. 'And maybe there's a leak in one of the pipes. There was dripping in there the whole time.'

'It's basically a death trap,' Hallie says. 'We should probably sue the school.'

'I will definitely get the leak looked into,' Mr Canton says. 'It's true that since the Latchitts disappeared, nothing gets fixed as quickly. Mr Latchitt would have had it sorted, lickety-split.' He looks around at all of us, and I mean *really* looks. He suspects something along the lines of the truth, or he knows something. I'm not sure which.

Colette wriggles in her chair.

'What's lickety spit?' Gus says. Trying to cover, I think. 'And how does it fix leaks? Sounds freaking disgusting.'

'Lickety-split, Mr Gustav,' Mr Canton says. 'It means in a jiffy.'

'Jiffy?' Naira says. 'Mr C, we can't understand what you're saying.'

'Quickly.' Mr Canton sighs. 'It means quickly. So, the three of you in the library – what happened there?'

'We sat looking at the sausage skin a while,' Gus says. 'Then when Hallie and Angelo didn't come back, we decided to go look for them.'

'So we logged off the computer, grabbed all our stuff, and went to leave,' Colette says.

'The side door was locked, which was strange, because Hallie and Angelo both left that way,' says Naira. 'So we tried the main door, and that was locked too. Or stuck.'

'I have a fear of enclosed spaces,' Colette says. 'And I started to freak out.'

'I didn't know that about you, Colette.'

Mr Canton puts down his cup. 'I'm sorry to hear that. The library is enormous, though. I wouldn't have thought it would bring on claustrophobia so quickly.'

'It's not the size of the space that counts,' Colette says, without missing a beat. 'It's the fact that it's enclosed and I can't get out. I panic whenever I'm trapped anywhere, no matter what size it is.'

'Oh, I see,' Mr Canton says. 'So you panicked?'

'And I hit the fire alarm,' Colette says. 'I'm sorry. I didn't mean to cause a massive drama, I was just desperate to get out.'

'Understandable, given the circumstances,' Mr Canton says. 'And thank you for telling me – saves me wasting a lot of time looking into how the alarm went off.'

'I believe that covers everything,' Hallie says. 'Can we go now?'

Mr Canton sits forward in his seat. 'Not just yet. I wanted a bit more information about what happened in the costume stores yesterday.

There was quite a lot of damage to a set of shelves, I believe?'

'I tripped,' Hallie says. 'I'm clumsy. Soz.'

Mr Canton sighs. 'Is there nothing else you want to tell me?'

I look at my feet so I won't make eye contact with the others.

'Right. Here's what we're going to do,' Mr C says. 'You guys are a tight-knit super-team, and that makes me so proud. Individually, you are brilliant humans, and together?' He throws up his arms and gestures at all of us. 'Together you are a force. I think you need some time to chat amongst yourselves – a debrief, if you will – to get yourselves hashtag "Back On Track". So I'm going to leave you here for half an hour. Put your feet up, have another hot choccie, Netflix and chill . . .' We all cringe into our seats. 'And talk to each other. But think about what I've said. If there's something going on, I'm here to help.' He smiles around at us, stands up, dusts off his trousers and leaves the room, closing the door behind him.

'Tell us,' Naira says. 'What the hell happened?'

'I was in the toilets when the app went off,' Hallie says. 'I didn't know what to do. I still felt sick. So I decided to stay locked in my cubicle and wait it out.'

'But she wasn't alone in the toilets,' I say. I tell them about the moment Mr Latchitt's feet stepped down behind the gap in the door. The memory of it makes me shudder.

'He must have been sitting on the toilet with his feet up,' Gus says. 'Or maybe he'd been bracing against the walls while he tried to push out a giant poo.'

'Gus!' Naira throws a cushion at him.

'What?' Gus says. 'I bet his poos are the size of bricks – a guy that girthy.'

'Gus!' Colette squeaks, but she's shaking with laughter.

'Don't tell me you weren't thinking it too,' Gus grins.

'No one else was thinking it, Gus,' Hallie says,

and she's trying really hard not to crack up with laughter.

'Seriously?' Gus says. 'Angelo, you were thinking it, right?'

I shake my head and manage to splutter out, 'Just you, man.'

We're all laughing, and then Gus says, 'It's my condition. It gives me poo envy.' And we lose it completely. It takes a few minutes for us to calm down enough to talk, but when we do, the words come easier. I can tell my part without dread creeping through my body. Hal can tell hers without needing to puke. The horror seems further away than it did a moment ago.

'Let me check your leg, Angelo,' Colette says. 'We should clean it at least.'

My leg is a scraped-up mess. There's basically a strip of skin missing from just above my ankle to just below my knee. It's raw and bloody and it burns when we dab at it with wet paper towels.

'If you hadn't set the fire alarm off, we would

have been worm food,' Hallie says. 'They were surprised, and it was enough for them to leg it out of there.'

'Yeah,' I say. 'They plan everything so thoroughly they don't know what to do when something happens they don't expect. We can use that.'

'Use it how?' Naira asks.

'By doing the opposite of what they think we'll do. It's the only way we'll gain an advantage.'

'So are you thinking we should tell Mr Canton about Flinch?' Colette asks. 'I mean, I know it's social suicide if anyone finds out, but . . .' She goes to say something else. Closes her mouth again. Shrugs.

'It's too dangerous to keep playing,' Hallie says. And we all look at her in surprise. Hallie loves Flinch – it appeals to her inner rage and cunning. At the start it was her who made us all download the app.

We sit in silence for a moment. I'm sure the

others are thinking, like I am, about the consequences if we out the game, and the consequences if we don't.

'I've been thinking about the Flinch tune,' Naira says. 'And wondering if there's more to it than just an annoying nursery rhyme that gets stuck in everyone's heads. The spider song from last time wasn't just a song, was it? It was a way for the Latchitts to control the spiders.'

'You could be on to something,' I say. 'The Latchitts don't do coincidences. But what are they controlling with the Flinch tune?'

'The obvious answer to that would be the worms,' Naira says. 'But we've only seen two of them – three if you count Michelle's – so unless they're hidden around the school doing things we don't know about yet, what would be the point?'

'Any chance they're using the tune to control us?' Colette says. 'When the app goes off, it's like my brain and body totally switch modes, from normal to insanely pumped on adrenaline in just a couple of seconds. I thought it was just Flinch build-up, but maybe there's more to it than that.'

'Yeah,' says Gus. 'It's like my body's full of . . .'

'Bees,' I say. 'Buzzing, humming, stinging bees.'

'Mine are more like butterflies,' Hallie says. 'I mean, I get hyped, but I'm not sure it's much different than I get about a hundred times a day in normal life.'

Naira smiles. 'Well, you are a constant smouldering fire of anger and vengeance.'

'True,' Hallie says.

'So there's a lot we don't know,' I say. 'But do we agree that allowing the Latchitts to control us with the game needs to stop?'

'Yes. It's making me paranoid. I'm on edge the whole time, and I'm being a stroppy cow.' Naira looks at me with a grin. 'Knowing the Latchitts are behind it – because they *must* be behind it – we'd be insane to keep playing.'

'Should we just delete it from our phones

then?' Gus says. 'I mean, do we need to bring the whole thing down and risk being Dread Wood High's most hated for the rest of our lives?'

'We could try it that way,' I say.

'But as long as people are playing, the Latchitts will use the game to sneak into school and get up to god knows what without anyone noticing.' Hallie takes the cold pack off her face. 'We'd still be in danger all the time.'

'Look what they did to both of you,' Colette says. 'You've been properly hurt. And even though they're targeting us, we don't know that they're not a threat to everyone else too. The game needs to be over and gone.'

I nod. 'Yeah. We need to properly get rid.'

'Agreed,' Hallie says.

'Same,' Naira says.

'Yeah,' Gus says. 'But how? And without the whole school hating us?'

'We let someone else do it,' I say. 'Someone who won't mind being blamed.'

There's a knock on the door, and Mr Canton

bounds into the room, like he's having the best day ever and hasn't wasted half his morning sorting us out.

'Happy to see you all looking much brighter.' He beams at us. 'How are you all feeling now? Good chat?'

We all look around at each other. Mr Canton is the obvious solution here, but he *is* a teacher, and nobody wants to be the one to drop us all in the scrat.

Mr Canton closes the door and sits down with us again. 'Look,' he says. 'I know what I'm asking is huge. I may be ancient, but I still remember how it feels to be at high school, and I know the pressures it brings.'

'Daily beatings, going up chimneys and the bubonic plague?' Gus says.

Mr C splutters out a laugh. 'Very good, Gus, but I meant more along the lines of peer pressure, fitting in . . .'

'No offence, Mr C,' Hallie says. 'But we're not bothered about fitting in. We're bothered about not having people spit in our lunch every day for the next however many years we're stuck at this place.'

'Or posting private stuff about us on social media,' says Colette.

'Putting gum in our hair, throwing bleach at our clothes . . .' Naira says.

'Tripping us in the corridors, slamming us into the lockers . . .' says Gus.

'I hear you,' Mr Canton says. 'I do. But there is something going on in this school. Up until this week it's been a nuisance – disruptive more than anything. But now it appears it's becoming dangerous. Most of the pupils at school are behaving aggressively, and I've had several people fall asleep in my lessons. Which seems impossible, right?' He grins at us and wiggles his eyebrows. 'And here you all are this morning, in school early, three of you scared enough to set off the fire alarm, and two of you looking like you've done two rounds with Frank Bruno.'

Gus says, 'Who's . . .?'

'Ask your parents,' Mr C says. 'He's the OG.' We roll our eyes. 'My point is that whatever's going on is escalating, and I think you know that too. You are all brilliant humans – clever, and clued-up, and capable. I know that better than anyone. I also know you have decent morals and that you listen to your consciences. I'm asking you to listen to them now.'

Gus starts a slow clap, and we all join in.

'That was beautiful, sir.' Colette takes off her glasses to wipe away a fake tear, and we all burst out laughing, even Mr C.

'We hear you, Mr C,' I say. 'But . . .'

'Let me help you before you say anything else.' Mr C puts his hand up. 'I have noticed that whatever is happening centres mostly around more unsupervised times of day – before and after school, and during breaks and lunchtimes. I know, I'm like Sherlock Holmes with my Mind Castle.' We try not to start laughing again. 'So I'm going to be in my office at all those times over the coming days. Next to my phone – my direct line that is answered only by me, the number for which I have written on this Post-it.' He sticks a green sticky note on the table between us. 'If I were to receive a message on that number, tipping me off about something occurring on the school grounds, I would be ready to investigate immediately, and make it look like I just happened to be there. I would have no idea who gave me the information, and I would take full credit for resolving the situation, using the wonders of my Mind Castle.' He looks around at all of us again. 'You get me, fam?'

We all splutter into laughter again, and before we can say anything else, Mr C gets up and heads for the door. 'Right, you all seem fine to me. Colette, Naira and Gus, go back to your lessons, please. Hallie and Angelo, Mrs Parekh is waiting for you at the Primrose Room to give you a final check before you are free to go about your day. I was never here.'

He leaves the room and closes the door.

'So we're doing this, right?' I say, looking at the green sticky note on the table.

'Yeah.' Naira peels it off the surface and holds it between her thumb and one finger like it might bite her. 'Who wants to look after the number?'

'I'll lose it,' Gus says, which is true.

'I'll take it,' Colette says. 'I'm good at keeping things hidden.'

I pretend not to notice Naira raising an eyebrow – I don't have the energy to get into it with her now.

'Thanks, Col,' I say. The others too.

'When do you reckon the next round will be?' Hallie says, picking up the cold pack and her bag.

'The Latchitts aren't giving us any breathing space.' I wince as I pick up my backpack. My hand, leg and face all hurt. 'They don't want us to have any recovery time between their attacks. Maybe so we don't have a chance to try to work out what they're up to or what we can do about it. I think there will be another round today.'

We leave the room separately, Hallie and me last of all. I feel the weight of my phone in my pocket – the threat of it like a ticking bomb.

CHAPTER SIXTEEN

TAKING CONTROL

First break is Flinch free. We do everything as we usually would – sitting together in the dining hall with our food so the rest of the year can see we're the same as we were yesterday, and the day before that. Hallie and I get some questions about our faces, and we laugh and say we were messing around and collided. No drama. People stop asking once word gets round that it wasn't anything interesting.

But there's a thought in my head that won't go away. I keep it to myself all morning, and it grows. Every time I move my leg and feel the open wound sticking painfully to the fabric of my trousers, knowing I'll have to peel them off it later, taking even more skin with them. Every time I talk, or laugh, and the lower half of my face throbs. Or I take a sip of drink and it stings the cuts in my mouth. When I pick up my bag and almost yelp because my hand is so bruised and swollen that it can't bear the weight of a backpack. Every time I look at the purple lump above Hallie's eye. Every time I catch Colette looking over her shoulder and then trying to disguise the fact that she's afraid. It grows.

'It's not enough to wait for the game to start, call in reinforcements and then hide,' I say, as we walk through the quad towards the classroom block after break. 'We need to take control.'

'Yes!' says Hallie. 'Always happy to seize back the power. But how do you mean?'

'We play,' I say. 'We make the call, drop the tip-off, and then we play Flinch.'

'Are you insane?' Colette says. 'Why?'

'It will take suspicion away from us if we join in the game properly,' Naira agrees. 'We need to get caught playing, the same as everyone else.'

'There's that,' I say. 'But it's also an opportunity. They expect us to run and hide from them – that's how they have it planned out. So we turn the tables.'

'We go looking for them?' Gus says.

I nod. 'We go looking for them. There are five of us, against two Latchitts. We'll know that help is on the way and there's no chance they'll stick around to get caught by a bunch of teachers, so they *will* run at some point. And until then, we could try to get some answers.'

'Mrs Latchitt does love to talk,' Hallie says.

'And they won't be expecting it,' says Gus. 'They'll be caught off guard.'

Colette stops walking. 'You can't be serious. Think about what you're suggesting here!

It's too dangerous. Look what they did to you this morning.'

'Because they had the jump on us,' I say.

'And we were split,' Naira says. 'They locked us in the library so it would just be two against two in the toilets. If we stay together . . .'

'And it will only be for a couple of minutes at the most,' I say. 'Then a mob of teachers will show up and shut it all down.'

'What if they lock us in somewhere again?' Colette says.

'Look, we don't know how they choose when or where Flinch will happen . . .' We've all stopped walking now. It's quiet in the quad and the sun is trying to shine between wispy clouds. 'But Mr C was right. It's mostly before or after school, or at lunch. Let's make sure we're close to places where we can't get locked in.'

'We choose the arena,' Gus says.

'The Dread Wood,' I say. 'It has to be. There are so many ways to run. They can't corner us in there.'

'But I freaking hate the freaking Dread Wood,' Naira says.

'I know,' I say. 'But we've escaped from it twice now, Nai. Once from the Latchitts, and once from three spider monsters. We can do this.'

Hallie is bouncing up and down on her feet like we're planning a trip to the fair. 'So we keep together the whole time we're not in class. And we stay out on the field.'

'And hope it doesn't rain,' Naira says.

'It's not going to rain, Naira.' Gus puts an arm around her. 'Look at that sky. Fate is on our side.'

'We stop hiding, and we turn this situation to our advantage,' I say. 'Everyone in?'

'So in,' Hallie says.

Gus nods. 'Me too.'

'I guess,' Naira huffs.

'Colette?' I say.

'All right,' she says, though she doesn't look happy about it. 'I'll save the number on my phone so we can call straight away. It'll only take five or ten minutes for the teachers to come, right?'

'Exactly,' I say. 'Mr Canton will be there. I'm sure of it.'

'OK then, I'm in too. I want an end to all this.'

We start walking again, and I feel better. Because we're doing something. Because Colette trusts me.

It's not until the dreg end of lunchtime that the Flinch app sounds. We're in the pig yard. Reggie and Theo are having a lazy day, lounging on the woodchip, letting out the odd snore.

'I could just lie down right here and fall asleep,' Colette says. She's sitting on the ground, stroking Theo's hairy back.

'Yeah,' I say. Klaus has trotted over for a tickle and a hug, and there's genuinely nothing I'd rather be doing right now. 'I'd be up for that. I love spending time with these guys.'

Naira and Gus are sitting on a stump. Naira has her knees pulled up, her head resting on them and her eyes closed, and Gus is stacking woodchips into towers. Hallie is cross-legged on the ground, brushing Candice who is grunting like she's living her best life. It's the most relaxed I've seen everyone for days. Makes sense that this is the moment the Latchitts choose to launch the next round on us.

It takes less than a second for us to move. Hallie and Colette run into the storage building next to the sty with the buckets and brushes we've been using. They'll make the call from there where no one can see them. The rest of us run to the gate where we wait, looking as impatient as we can, and watch about thirty other Year 7s disappearing into the Dread Wood.

The tune has finished by the time Hallie and Colette come running out of the stores to meet us at the gate.

'Let's go,' Colette says.

We leave the pig yard, making sure the gate is shut behind us, then we plunge into the trees. This is it.

CHAPTER SEVENTEEN

WE PLAY

As soon as we're in the wood, the atmosphere changes. The shade of the trees makes everything colder and darker than it was on the field. The breeze makes the branches rustle and whisper. I feel eyes on me.

Being in a team of five means it's almost impossible for us to move through the woods without being seen and heard, but it also means many players will let us pass by, rather than trying to take us on. I take the lead. I know the woods best out of all of us.

We have a plan for the Latchitts – a plan that will hopefully lead to us getting answers to some of our questions – and that's at the front of my mind. But we also need to make it look like we're playing the game, and the best way to do that is to actually play. So I focus on getting a flinch.

The bush where Naira hid is a good place to start. As we approach it from the main path, we pretend we can't see Mariam and Zaynab hiding inside. We pass it, then I circle back while they're watching the others. I come at it from behind, and I roar. Two screams. Easy Flinch points. I collect one on my phone, and I let Gus have the other because he did an excellent job of keeping their eyes on him by doing a weird walk on the path.

Mariam and Zaynab run off. Points in the bag, we turn away from the path and head deeper into the Dread Wood. Colette scores a point by jumping and swinging on a low branch that Liam Dander was hiding on. As cover, it's enough. We focus on getting ourselves away from the rest of the players, on making ourselves vulnerable, so the Latchitts will make a move.

We're by the boundary fence when I catch a flash of movement out of the corner of my eye. I stop. 'Did you see that?' I whisper to the others.

They all stop and turn to look at the trees behind us. Everything is still.

'I didn't see anything,' Naira says.

I shrug and we start moving again. Another twenty metres along, I hear something – a twig snapping as it's stepped on. It's a noob move and not one the Latchitts would make unless it was deliberate. I wonder if they're messing with us. Time for us all to get into character and play the different parts we planned. I spin around.

'I'm telling you there's someone there,' I say.

Colette puts her hand up. 'I actually heard something that time.'

'Told you,' I say to the others.

Naira tuts. 'So what are we doing about it?'

'Hold on,' Gus says. 'Why does Angelo always get to decide the plan? I don't get it.' He gives me a look. 'No offence.'

Naira shrugs. 'He knows the woods best. And he's good at tactics.'

'Is he, though?' Gus says. 'Because last time I was with him for a round of Flinch, we got attacked by a creepy-ass scarecrow and then locked in a cupboard.'

I feel my temper flare – I can't help it. Even though we agreed to this and I know it's all part of the plan, it's like I can't flatten those bees inside.

'I'd like to see you do any better,' I say. 'All you're good for is screaming like an extra in a low-grade zombie movie.'

'That's harsh, man,' Gus says. He does a good job of looking hurt.

'How's this?' Hallie says. 'I'll be in charge.'

'Why you?' I say.

'Because you had your chance, like Gus said. I ended up with a smashed face. I'm not doing what you say any more.'

Naira glares at Hallie. 'It wasn't Angelo's fault. If you hadn't gone running off in the first place, he wouldn't have ended up looking like this.' She points at my chin and lip.

'Guys,' Colette squeaks. 'This sucks. Let's just split up and play separately. Angelo and Naira, you clearly want to work together . . .' She gives us the dirtiest look. 'So go do your own thing. We'll carry on with three of us.'

I try not to be hurt that she's so good at pretending to be mad with me.

'Fine,' I say, storming ahead. Naira follows me.

'We'll do better without you,' Hallie shouts after us.

I don't turn around.

Nai and I keep walking by the fence, next to the train tracks. We move as silently as we can, and I concentrate on being aware of any noise or movements around me. I try to keep my breathing quiet and steady. I try to ignore every itch and urge to cough.

We've not gone far before I'm as certain as I can be that this part of the Dread Wood is empty, except for us and a couple of squirrels. Whoever was behind us has gone – most likely after the others. I stop for a moment. Exchange a look with Naira. Then we turn and head away from the boundary, towards the clearing. Because if we're going to have a stand-off with the Latchitts then there's only one place in these woods where it's going to be. The Arena of Eternal Horror.

As we approach the clearing, I hear it: whistling. Mr Latchitt. And then voices – Hallie's first, shouting some abuse in standard Hallie style. Mrs Latchitt giggles. She would have been waiting there like before, while Mr Latchitt followed the others to block the path behind them. Gus and Colette will be between them, where Naira and I stood a few days ago. I wonder why Mr Latchitt made that choice, to follow the other three, and not me and Naira. I put it away for later. We don't have much time.

Nai and I move in from the side of the clearing nearest the boundary fence. If we've got this right, when we step out of the trees, we'll have a perfect view of everyone else. Nai gives my hand a squeeze, then we separate out a few metres – close enough to be able to move back together quickly if we need to, but far enough to give the Latchitts two extra places to try to keep their eyes on.

We take the last few paces quickly, and stride into the clearing. Hallie, Gus and Col are in place, and the Latchitts are where we hoped they'd be. They're in their jack-in-the-box masks, of course. They turn towards us like they're surprised, and I try to ignore the smug feeling that surges up inside me. Don't get cocky, Angelo.

'Wily fox has come to play,' Mrs Latchitt says. 'And with so many wounds to lick.'

Hal, Gus and Colette space out a bit. Stand taller. The Latchitts look around – five to two now, their faces turned to Colette for longer than they glance at the rest of us – and Mr Latchitt takes the smallest of steps backwards.

'What do you want from us?' I ask. 'Why do you keep coming back?'

'You have a treasure you don't deserve,' Mrs Latchitt says, her masked face snapping from Colette to me.

'And we have mouths to feed,' Mr Latchitt snarls. It's the first time I've heard him talk since back in the basement lab, and I'd forgotten how menacing his voice is, like he's caging a truckload of rage under the thinnest layer of forced calm.

'You mean your worms,' Hallie says. 'What's the point?'

Mr Latchitt turns to her. 'They're so much more than worms. Both in form and in ambition.'

'We had this exact same conversation,' Gus says. 'Do you have a name for them, by any chance? Asking for a friend.'

Mrs Latchitt tilts her head. 'They're my little

famished ones. Hungry, hungry, always hungry.'

'"Little famished ones",' Gus says. 'Not very catchy. I'd keep thinking if I were you.'

'Hungry for what?' I ask.

'Don't you know?' Mrs Latchitt giggles. 'My famished ones eat fear. They gorge themselves on it. They eat, then they sleep. Eat and sleep, eat and sleep, eat and sleep.'

'And they're never full,' Mr Latchitt says. 'They'll keep taking what they need.'

'Wake up, sleepy-heads!' Mrs Latchitt squeals. 'Breakfast time!'

Colette looks from Mrs Latchitt to Mr Latchitt, then back again. 'So what, are you going to infect everyone?'

'Everyone is riddled with guilt, like maggoty apples,' Mrs Latchitt says. She looks hungrily at Colette. 'Even you, my sweetling, choosing to befriend those we toiled so fiercely to punish just for you.'

'So is this about Colette?' Naira asks. 'Or because we blew up your spiders?'

'The story started long before that,' Mrs Latchitt says. 'We discovered the land. We prepared the soil. We planted seeds. And now we're watching them flourish and thrive. There are those who'll pay a pretty penny for our precious babies, but only if we prove their worth.'

'You're testing your worms out on us?' Hallie says. 'So you can sell them?'

'Science requires funding. And who better than you, little piggies?' Mrs Latchitt says. 'We know you. We know this school, this town. It couldn't be more perfect. You should be honoured.' She claps her hands and smiles.

'Not really feeling the love tbh,' Gus says. 'I mean, I'd be OK if you tested them somewhere else.'

'And we don't like you,' Mr Latchitt bellows like a raging bear.

There's a second of silence, and then the shrill sound of a whistle splitting the air.

Mr and Mrs Latchitt look towards the field

where the sound came from. There are more whistles, sharp and unnatural sounding here in the Dread Wood. It's PE whistles being blown, and by lots of different people. Mr Canton has brought backup.

'They'll be looking for us,' Hallie says. 'So really sorry to leave this crazy chat, but we have to go.'

The whistles are getting closer, moving through the woods.

The Latchitts look at each other and then turn towards the fence, moving faster than I've ever seen them. They're scared. They can't risk getting caught.

Naira and I run towards the others and we all turn in the opposite direction.

'You'll need us when your weasel goes *pop*,' Mrs Latchitt calls after us, but she's looking at Colette.

We jog through the trees, no time to talk about what just happened. Right now we need to seem like every other Year 7 – gutted that we've been caught out, and bracing ourselves for the trouble ahead. As we leave the trees, the Flinch app sounds for the end of the game. Kids are running out of the woods and being rounded up by about fifteen teachers with whistles and their most furious teacher faces.

'You five, over here now,' Mr Canton shouts across the field. I feel like it must be taking everything in him to not give us a cheeky wink but, to his credit, he manages to play it like we're just another bunch of kids caught doing something really, really bad. We walk over and sit on the grass with everyone else, exchanging looks and then keeping our heads down whenever a teacher looks our way.

Though on the outside I must look shaken, on the inside it's a different story. My pounding heart starts to slow. The buzz of the bees fades away. My twitching muscles relax. I know this isn't over. But it feels like, for the first time since Flinch started, we've gained a point worth scoring.

CHAPTER EIGHTEEN

GAME OVER

The whole school is called into an assembly later that afternoon. It's been a long day, and I'm aching to go home. I'm hoping that what's said in the next fifteen minutes will mean I can actually rest when I get there. We file into the hall and down the rows of plastic chairs which are all linked together so you're uncomfortably close to the people next to you. There's normally a bit of chat and mucking around when we do this, but today is different. There are teachers shooting daggers at anyone who even breathes too loudly, and an air of 'something big is going to happen' that makes everyone nervous.

Mr Hume, the head teacher, steps out on to the stage.

'They've released the kraken!' I hear Gus say from a couple of rows behind me, and a bunch of people laugh, covering it with coughs and nose-blows. Colette is next to me, and I can see her biting her lip so she doesn't giggle.

'Good afternoon, Dread Wood pupils,' Mr Hume says, his voice booming around the hall. 'I know it's unusual for us to gather for an assembly this late in the day, and that it's been a very long day for many of you, so I will keep this brief.'

I feel the whole school eye-roll. He won't keep it brief.

'The school staff at Dread Wood High are the most committed and conscientious team that I, as a head, could wish for. Their focus on your development, as learners and as people, is hawk-like. As such, it will not come as a surprise for you to learn that we became aware of

216

something untoward happening in this school several weeks ago. I'm sure many of you . . .' He stares around at all of us, pausing to make eye contact with quite a few people. I'm sure I would have been one of them if I hadn't taken up the role of school snitch. '*Many* of you know exactly what I'm referring to, while others, perhaps, are in the dark.'

Literally everyone knows what he's talking about.

'There is a game that has become popular with Dread Wood pupils during the past month. It involves downloading a mobile telephone application, known as the Flinch app, which sends alerts to players to let them know that a game is under way and that they must play. The game involves scaring other players to force a reaction, or "*flinch*" . . .' he actually does the fingers, 'from them.' He pauses. Looks around again. Watches faces.

'Not only is this game irresponsible in its entire concept – scaring other pupils is unacceptable behaviour at any time – but its implications are incredibly dangerous. This is a game that could lead to serious injury. I'm sure many of you are already harbouring cuts and bruises . . .' Dramatic pause again to make us all feel the full pain of those cuts and bruises. 'It is only a matter of time before a far graver injury occurs. Perhaps a broken bone, perhaps a concussion, perhaps worse.'

I count the seconds of his silence this time – sixteen of them. Feels more like five minutes.

'In addition, our technical whizzes have been analysing the Flinch application, and what you probably don't know – and make sure you listen extremely carefully to this – is that the application, which originates at an unknown source, is accessing personal and private data from your phones. It is tracking your movements, through GPS location software. It knows exactly where you are at all times.'

I feel Colette tense beside me. How did we not think of that? The Latchitts have been ten steps ahead of us, because they always know where we are.

'At Dread Wood High, we discuss internet safety with every pupil regularly and thoroughly, so I am disappointed that many of you have chosen to ignore the guidance that is in place FOR YOUR PROTECTION.' Another hard stare. 'Discussions about this will be continuing over the coming weeks. Every student will attend sessions on internet safety until we are absolutely certain that lessons have been learned.' Pause, glare, take a breath. 'And in the meantime, we have an issue that needs to be dealt with swiftly and with full force.'

I swear I can feel everyone in the room hold their breath.

'A letter has been sent to the parents or guardians of every Dread Wood High student this afternoon. Parents have been asked to respond to confirm that they have read the contents and that they agree to support our plan of action. Parents who don't respond will be telephoned until they do. In short – there is no avoiding this matter for any of you. We are treating this situation with the utmost urgency and seriousness, and any pupil found to be breaking the following rules will feel the full weight of their actions.'

Here it comes, finally.

'Between leaving this assembly and returning to school tomorrow morning, those of you with the Flinch app on your mobile phone will delete it fully. During registration tomorrow, your form tutors will be checking your mobile phones to ensure that there is no trace of the application. And for those of you who are perhaps already planning ways around this, be aware that Dread Wood staff are receiving extensive training to prevent anything from slipping past them unnoticed. We. Will. Not. Be. Hoodwinked.'

If this was about anything else, I'd be as outraged as Hallie about the infringement of my rights and privacy. As it is, I'm relieved. So relieved.

'We will be performing random spot checks from tomorrow morning. If any of you re-download the Flinch app, we will find out, and there will be consequences. On Friday evening, the much anticipated Dread Wood High celebrations at Finches Green fair are due to take place. I know many of you are looking forward to it. Anyone found with the application on their phone before that time will be banned from attending.

On entry to the fair on Friday, Dread Wood staff will be checking all mobile phones to ensure the application is not present, and should it be found on your phone you will be refused entry. This is non-negotiable. There are no loopholes or exceptions. Do not test us. You will be sorry that you did.'

Pause – twenty seconds this time. Too long because the teachers start looking at each other like they're not sure if they should be filing us out or waiting.

'Now,' Mr Hume says, and everyone jumps.

221

'Let us get back to making Dread Wood High a
school to be proud of, focusing on our values of
teamwork, respect, attitude, curiosity and
kindness. Flinch is behind us, and there it will
remain.'

CHAPTER NINETEEN

SLEEP, WAKE, EAT

We're sent straight home from school after assembly. The five of us huddle together by the school car park, holding our phones so that they glow in the shadowy space between us, and we delete the Flinch app together. It feels like a weird ceremony. Then Hallie and Gus get a lift with Colette, and Naira and I walk home together. It honestly feels like days since we last made this same journey, but in the opposite direction.

'Well *that* was a day,' Naira says.

I glance across at her. Perfectly neat and tidy and uniform fully intact, unlike mine which is torn in a couple of places and covered with dirt. 'And even with everything that happened, you still look like a swot on school photo day.' I nudge her gently with my elbow to show I'm messing with her, just in case. Our argument this morning made me feel like a heap of burning trash.

She smiles. 'Swot on school photo day is my whole vibe. I've spent years working on it.' She glances back at me. 'You look wrecked.'

'Yeah,' I snort. 'Well, wrecked is my vibe.'

'How are your wounds?' Naira asks. 'No offence, but they make you look nasty.'

'Hurt like hell, actually. But, you know, could be worse.'

'Do you think it's over?' Naira says.

The roads are busy with after-school traffic and kids walking home in their usual groups. Shaheed, Mo and Kai going into the shop on the corner, and the owner shouting at them to wait because there are already three kids in there and he has a strict 'four Dread Wood kids at a time' limit. Some parent arguing out of their window with a traffic warden while they wait on the double yellows for their kid to come out. Bikes whizzing past. Car horns. The smell of diesel, vape fumes and cold spring air. Chatting between friends that I can't make out because of all the street noise, except for the odd shouted word. There's less laughing – everyone's gutted about the end of Flinch, but other than that, all normal things.

And yet. 'Honestly, I don't believe the Latchitts will just give up. We might have bought some time, but they'll be back.'

'The things they said in the woods,' Naira says. 'They didn't make much sense, but surely we can work some of it out. It could help.'

I nod. 'There was the stuff about the worms. That they eat fear. What the hell does that mean?'

'That she's even more twisted than she was in November,' says Naira. 'But it did confirm that the worms are eating something. Always hungry, remember? They feed off something inside the body.'

'But not food,' I say. 'Because they don't live in the stomach.'

Naira frowns. 'So what could it be?'

'I don't know. Something they get from puncturing the brain, maybe? Or they could absorb a substance or chemical from the blood.'

'Grim.'

'They sleep, wake and eat. Then go back to sleep again, so they're not active all the time.'

'Hal said Michelle was mostly normal before that freak-out when we were over,' Naira says. 'So maybe her worm was sleeping.'

'And something woke it up,' I say. 'That fits.'

'This is good. Feels like we're getting somewhere.'

I mean, it's not much, but it's something. And we need to feel like things aren't completely hopeless, like we can have some say over what happens from this point on.

'They said they planted seeds long ago, which I think must mean infecting the chickens with the parasites to grow them or breed them, or whatever you call it when you're creating an army of brain-biting worms.'

'Yes,' Naira says. 'Do you think all the chickens had them?'

'Probably.'

'But they were happy to let their spider babies eat the chickens which you'd think would pass the parasites on. They really loved those spiders – surely they wouldn't have wanted to infect them?'

'Unless,' I say, 'the worms aren't harmful to spiders. Maybe they can't get the food they need from them.'

'Which narrows down what the worms are feeding on. Something they can get from chickens and humans, but not spiders.'

'I'll do some research,' I say. 'Promise I won't fall asleep this time.'

We turn off the main road and on to the side streets that lead to our estate.

'It was like those words about planting seeds had a double meaning,' I say. 'There's a bigger plan going on than just ruining our lives.'

'They want to sell their creations,' Naira says. 'But to who? The people funding their experiments?'

'Maybe they want to sell the Flinch app too,' I add.

Naira's eyes widen. 'Imagine if their creatures were used on a bigger scale, like to control a whole town, or even a country?'

'Like if they were owned by the military or a corrupt government or something?' I say. 'That's insane. Like potentially end-of-the-world-apocalypse insane.'

'Yeah. But the Latchitts *are* insane, and there are some really awful people in the world who'll do anything for power.'

'Is it possible that we're the origin story for the biggest of bads?'

'I guess we'll have to find out.'

'Yeah,' I say, but my head can't take it in.

Naira side-eyes me. 'You know when Mrs Latchitt said the thing about needing them when the weasel goes pop?'

'Yeah,' I sigh. 'No idea what she was talking about.'

'Did you feel like she was saying it to all of us?' Naira says. 'Because I thought it was intended just for . . .'

'Colette,' I say. 'You still have beef with her?'

'Not beef,' Naira says. 'But isn't it strange that the Latchitts have come at all of us, except for her? The worst they did was lock her in the library – big deal – and they didn't even throw a worm in with her.'

'So maybe they don't want to infect her,' I say. 'They're her grandparents, and we know how protective they are of her. Just because they don't hate her like they hate us, it doesn't mean she's somehow working with them. If that's what you're saying?' I turn to look at

Naira, but she keeps her eyes on the pavement.

'You're right,' she says, after a pause. 'It's probably just that. Like I said earlier, I'm angry and suspicious all the time. I don't trust my own judgement any more.'

I'm annoyed that she's still thinking scrat about Colette, and a huge part of me wants to go at her again. But I bite it down. I don't want another fight.

'So popping the weasel,' I say. 'Obviously that's a reference to the nursery rhyme, but does it mean something more literal too? I wish Ma Latchitt wouldn't talk in riddles all the time.'

'Same. And I'm so sick of that awful tune.'

'Hell, yes,' I say. 'If I ever have kids, they're going to be raised on more wholesome music, like gangster rap and death metal.'

Naira nods. 'Let's hope your research turns up some answers.'

'Most likely I'll find more questions. But it's worth a try.'

As we turn into our estate, a wave of

tiredness and relief rushes through me, so strong that my legs almost give way. I could honestly just sit on the concrete looking up at our flat and stay there until someone comes looking for me.

'Just one thing,' Naira says, before we go our separate ways. 'If you discover anything, don't message it to the rest of us. Save it for tomorrow.'

'You're thinking about the Latchitts' having access to our phones,' I say.

'I am. I know we've deleted the app, and they probably couldn't see our messages anyway. But just in case.'

I nod. 'Yeah, just in case.'

We say goodbye and I climb the steps to home, my legs throbbing and my back aching. Mum's waiting for me at the door, and I know I'm going to have some explaining to do before I can get on the computer.

It's hours later, after talking with Mum, playing with Raph, eating dinner, and then explaining everything again to Dad when he gets home that I finally get a chance to do some research. My eyes are burning in their sockets, the lids drooping. Raph is breathing deeply in his sleep, curled like a peanut in a shell on the top bunk. The room is full of galaxies, shining from his starlight projector. I want so badly to crawl into bed, but I can't let the others down.

I open the busted-up laptop and try to get my brain into gear while I listen to it painfully chugging to life. Where do I start? Mrs Latchitt's words come back to me. Fear. The worms feed on fear. I type 'fear in the body' into the search box and scroll through the results, not expecting to find much. But my eyes fall on a page from a medical website, and, almost before I click on it, the threads start connecting in my mind.

Feeding on fear.

I don't know why I didn't think of it before.

CHAPTER TWENTY

SKIN AND TEETH

I have to wait until first break to share what I've learned with the others. It's one of those days that makes you feel that warmer days are ahead. The sky is pale blue, with wisps of fluffy white cloud, and though the sun isn't hot, it's warm enough to feel. We take our food out to the field and sit on the wall of the pig yard. Everything at Dread Wood High feels different today – quieter, calmer, like the sharp edges have been rubbed off. People are going back to their pre-Flinch business.

'How's Michelle?' I ask Hallie.

Hallie's face is even more colourful today than it was yesterday, with the bruise blossoming across her skin. 'She's stable, but they can't work out how to get rid of the worm. They've tried the usual worming treatments, medications and stuff, but they haven't worked. They're going to try a surgical procedure today.'

'Are you worried?' Colette says.

'Yeah, I am. Seems drastic having to cut her open.'

'Remember she's a tough little chicken,' Gus says. 'She's survived monster spiders and being thrown down a well. She can survive this.'

'I hope so,' Hallie says. She smiles. 'She's such a queen.'

I swallow a mouthful of sausage roll. 'Has the worm got any bigger? Or done anything different?'

'No, they said it's barely moved, and possibly got a little smaller. It's tricky to tell because of the way it's, you know, wrapped around her bones. Why?' Hallie sips her smoothie. It's the same colour as her bruise.

'Because I think I have something,' I say. 'I managed to do some research last night – shut up Naira . . .' I add because I can see she's opening her mouth to make a comment about me falling asleep again. 'And I'm ninety per cent sure that the worms feed on adrenaline.'

'The stuff your body makes when you're pumped up?' Gus asks.

'Exactly. When you're scared or whatever, your adrenal gland releases adrenaline into your bloodstream to help you deal with it.'

'They feed on fear,' Naira says.

'And the response is all triggered from a part of the brain that sends messages through your nervous system to your endocrine system.'

'Your what?' Colette asks.

'It's boring and complicated, and I can go through it all if you want me to, but basically it would explain why the worm is latching on to

Michelle's brain.' I explain. 'It's trying to control that whole chain of fear, leading to the adrenaline rush.'

'Like milking a cow,' Gus says. 'The worm is milking her brain.'

'That's disgusting.' Hallie throws a piece of lettuce at him.

'But a weirdly good way of describing it,' I say. 'When the worm is awake, it presses on the part of the brain that will lead to the adrenaline being released . . .'

'The udders, if you will,' Gus says.

'. . . right. Then it feeds on the adrenaline.'

'Angelo, you're a genius,' Colette says. 'That's got to be it.'

'So the worm in Michelle is milking her?' Hallie asks. 'And it gets bigger every time she's scared?'

'I think so,' I say. 'But spiders don't have the same anatomy, so munching on parasitic chicken wouldn't affect them.'

'But how come I only saw her freak out that one time?' Hallie says. 'I spend loads of time with her and she's never done it before. Only when you were over.'

'. . . and we were arguing over whether to play Flinch,' I say. 'Something must have triggered her.' I make a mental note to replay the scene in my mind next time I have the opportunity to think properly. Like when I'm bored in drama class. Maybe I can work out what freaked Michelle out so much.

'The important question right now, is how can this information help Michelle?' Hallie asks.

'I guess as long as she stays calm and happy, the parasite can't grow. It might even starve and die, though I have no idea how long that would take. I mean, chickens are nervy birds.' I knock back the last of my hot chocolate. 'And it's possible that the vet will find a way to kill the worm off even quicker.'

We sit in silence for a moment, watching the pigs snuffling around.

'Anyone else thought of anything that might help us?' I ask. 'I feel like there's loads we still don't know, and we're not going to feel safe anywhere until we can make a better guess at the Latchitts' next move.'

'*Anywhere*?' Gus says. 'I hope you're not suggesting that we swerve the fair on Friday. The fair is everything that is good and wholesome, and I won't hear of us abandoning it.'

'Have you seen the ghost train?' Naira says. 'There's nothing good or wholesome about that.'

'Because the fair is also seductive and mysterious,' Gus says. 'It's what makes it so irresistible – the sexy temptress.'

'Gross,' Naira says. 'And in answer to your question, Angelo, I had a search on the internet last night and found nothing. I was wondering if the masks could give us any clues about the Latchitts, but I found a few places where anyone can buy them online.'

'What?' Gus says. 'I thought they made those masks especially for us. How disappointing.'

'I guess they're too busy being evil genetic scientists,' Colette says. 'They don't have time to make special masks.'

'Evil genetic scientists need hobbies too, Colette,' Gus says. 'Everyone deserves some crafting time.'

'Yeah, what better way to relax of an evening than sitting in front of the fire, sewing creepy masks,' I say.

'Out of human skin and teeth,' Gus agrees.

'Guys, why does every conversation we have come back to cannibalism?' Hallie huffs.

'Hey, I said nothing about them eating the people whose skin and teeth they use,' Gus says. 'So *you're* the one making it about cannibalism, Hallie.'

'I thought the eating part was implied,' Hallie says.

Colette starts giggling. 'When is the eating of people ever implied?'

Naira grins. 'This says a lot about the state of our lives.'

'Hold on,' Hallie says. 'How are the teeth human when they're so pointy and fangy?'

Gus rolls his eyes. 'Obviously they file them into shape.'

'But then why not use shark or crocodile teeth instead and save themselves the bother?' I say. 'Pretty sure you can just buy them on eBay.'

'God, Angelo,' Gus says. 'The Latchitts are animal lovers. Think of the poor sharks and crocodiles, will you?'

'Sadly, that actually makes sense,' I say. 'Your mind is a wondrous place, Gustav.'

'You say wondrous, I say disturbing,' Naira says.

'The point is,' Gus says, standing up as the bell for next period rings out, 'that we are going to the fair on Friday. Flinch is gone. There will be an army of teachers there. The Latchitts are probably taking some time to relax and do some arts and crafts. It will be perfectly safe.'

We pick up our bags and start walking towards the classroom block. I want to believe that Gus is right – a night of fun sounds so appealing right now. The Latchitts are regrouping and we have to take our chances while we can. So I tell myself that if nothing bad happens between today and tomorrow night, then we're on.

We'll go to the fair, and then we'll deal with whatever comes next.

CHAPTER TWENTY-ONE

THE FEAR GROUND

O n Friday all anyone is talking about is the fair. Every kid in school is buzzing, and even some of the teachers too. It's hard not to get swept up in it, so I stop trying. The day passes with no signs of trouble, and by the time the final bell goes, Gus is literally bouncing around like a grasshopper in a jar.

'See you at six, yeah?' he says, as he gets in his dad's car. 'Don't be late, 'cos there will be queues to get in with all the phone-checking and shiz. And make sure you dress nice – the fair deserves our best efforts.' To be honest, I don't know how he's going to last until six without exploding.

At 5:40, Naira and I meet outside her flat, and walk up to the green together, talking about a hundred different things – anything except the Latchitts, though I'm sure they're lurking at the back of her mind like they are in mine.

As we approach Finches Green, we hear the fair before we see it – a mix of pop music and the sounds of the rides clamouring to be the loudest. It's still broad daylight, but the fair is lit up anyway, the rides rising up from behind the trees and bushes that surround the green.

Gus, Hallie and Colette are waiting for us at the entrance, looking up at the biggest rides, which are screaming against the green of the park in their neon colours and flashing lights.

There's a magic to seeing something so boring and everyday transformed this way. Usually Finches Green means school, and lessons, and teachers. But right now it means freedom, and fun, and . . .

'Ah, it's the fab five.' Mr Canton waves at us. 'And all looking drippin', I must say.'

. . . teachers.

'You just say "drippin'" on its own, Mr C, not "looking drippin'".' Hallie rolls her eyes.

'Or better still, maybe don't say it at all,' I add.

'All righty then.' Mr C grins. 'How about sick and dope?'

'Please stop, sir,' Gus says. 'It's embarrassing for all of us.'

Mr Canton laughs, and looks down a list on the clipboard he's holding. 'If you would kindly present your phones for inspection, we can get the checks out of the way and you will be free to enjoy an evening of tweenage revelry.'

We hand over our phones, one by one, while a

long line of Dread Wood students starts to build up behind us.

'You see,' Gus says, bouncing on his toes. 'Was I right about the queue or what? Good thing your homeboy Gustav made you get here early.'

'You are all clear,' Mr Canton says, handing back our phones and ticking us off his list. 'Now bear with me – I have to say this next bit before I can let you in . . . Please remember that while in attendance of this event, you are representatives of Dread Wood High, and as such we expect you to behave in a manner that reflects the school's high standards. You may not be wearing your uniform, but the school's key values should be at the front of your mind at all times.' He grins. 'Imagine them running through you like Brighton rock.'

'What's Brighton rock?' Hallie says.

'Hallie!' Gus squeaks. 'Why would you ask that when we were so close to getting away?'

'Brighton rock is a confectionery item made almost entirely of sugar,' Mr Canton says.

'It's shaped into a thin cylinder, about yea long . . .' He holds up his hands to show us. 'It's often striped on the outside and has words written on the inside that run through the length of the rock. Cheeky messages from yester-year are common, along the lines of "kiss me quick".'

We all visibly cringe.

'I'm so sorry,' Hallie says. 'I made a rookie error. Mr C, please stop.'

'Did I lose you at "kiss me quick"?' Mr Canton winks.

'It was yester-year for me,' Colette says.

'Yea long, here.' Gus puts his hand up.

'I think I was gone before you finished the words "Brighton rock",' I say.

'Naira.' Mr C turns to her. 'You're always down for some learning, am I right?'

She shakes her head. 'Not this time, Mr C. Sorry.'

'Well, if I've managed to bore even Naira, then I'd better let you be on your way. Have fun and stay safe.' He does a dramatic bow with a curly wave, and we finally walk past him on to the green. We hear him greet the next group of students in line like they're in for the same treatment we had, and then his voice is lost to the sound of the fair.

'I have the best news,' Hallie says, as we head towards the lights. 'Michelle defeated her parasite.'

'That *is* the best news,' Colette says.

'How did it happen?' I ask. 'Did the vet remove it during surgery?'

'That's the most brilliant part,' Hallie says. 'They didn't even get to the surgery. They were prepping Michelle, shaving the downy feathers off the back of her neck with an electric razor so they could make the incision or whatever. They had the scanner on so they could see inside while they surgeried, and just as they were about to go in, the worm spasmed and dropped off.'

'So it just let go?' Gus says.

'It let go, and the little son of a scrut dropped dead.'

'Michelle really is a queen,' Colette says.

Hallie grins. 'Right? What a warrior.'

'Not saying Michelle isn't a warrior queen,' Naira says. 'But I wonder if something caused it. Seems weird for it to just give up and die for no reason.'

'It knew it was messing with the wrong chicken,' Hallie says. 'Simple.'

I don't say anything because I don't want to burst Hallie's bubble, but I'm with Naira. Something must have triggered the spasming. It all needs thinking about, but now is not the time.

'Damn it, we're not first,' Gus says, seeing a few groups of Dread Wood kids already wandering around the green. 'They must have snuck in the other gate while Mr C was banging on about antique sweets. Your fault, Hallie.'

'To be fair,' I said. 'Our mistake was coming in at his gate. Miss Heeps is on the other one and she hates talking to students.'

Colette nods. 'Especially on Fridays.'

'Enough chit-chat,' Gus says. 'Give me your

money, and let's find a token machine.'

We all empty our pockets into Gus's open hands.

'Do we need to keep any back for anything?' Naira asks. 'Food and stuff?'

Gus sighs. 'No, Naira, we already talked about this. The currency of the fair is tokens. Your cash is no good here.'

'Unless you're using it to buy tokens,' I say.

'Don't be a smart-arse, Angelo. No one likes a smart-arse.'

'Especially Gustav in manic fair mode,' Colette says with a grin.

Gus leads us to a tattered marquee with open sides that's full of arcade games inviting us to do some underage gambling. In each corner is a token machine. It takes a while for us to feed our money in – we have a lot between us, though nobody bothers to count it – and wait for the tokens to spew out. They're plastic discs, about the size of ten pences, supposed to be golden, but scratched and worn by being used so much that they look like they've been chewed by a pack of rabid dogs.

'Why do they have "F"s embossed on them?' Colette asks.

'Because . . .' Gus rolls his eyes, 'F is the letter of freedom and fun, of fantastical freshness and festive fortune, of fragrant flirtatious favourites. F is fit. F is fabulous.'

'And also the first letter of "fair",' Naira says.

We all laugh, except Gus who is fully focused on scooping the tokens into a bumbag he bought especially for the occasion. 'Got the idea from Mr Canton and our phones in detention.' He zips it up and pats it with a smile. 'Nobody's getting their hands on these tokens without also getting uncomfortably close to my private parts.'

We step out of the arcade, back on to the green, and look around us. The sun is going down, the dusky sky making the lights of the fair seem to shine brighter. It's like we're standing in a different world. There's a city around us, full of shape and colour. Skyscrapers of rides reaching up to touch the clouds. Others spread low and wide across the covered grass, surrounded by battered railings. There are winding lanes of stalls selling snacks that fill the air with smells of candy floss, and fries, and popcorn. Shifty-looking huts and tents holding games of skill that are almost impossible to win. We'll try them all anyway. The fairground people stand quietly by the attractions, taking people's tokens and pressing buttons to stop and start the rides. They're dressed in dark clothing, and so still that they almost melt into the dusky background. It feels like the fair belongs to us and only us.

'Isn't she wonderful?' Gus says, opening his arms wide like he's the ringmaster of the world's greatest circus. 'Thank you for welcoming us, my lady fair, and allowing us to worship at your magical altar.'

'I'm not worshipping at anyone's altar,' Hallie says in disgust.

'Hush now, child, or the fair will hear you,'

Gus whispers. 'Do you know how her attractions are powered?'

'By the generators.' Naira points to a row of trailers lined up behind the rides, with enormous hunks of chugging metal on their backs.

'Wrong, Nai-Nai,' Gus says. 'They're powered by a particular kind of magic that only exists when we believe in the majesty of the fair.'

'No. They're powered by electricity from generators,' Naira sighs.

'What first?' I ask. Because this discussion could go on for ages.

'I took the liberty of making a priority list.' Gus pulls a piece of paper out of his pocket. 'Based on the average queue time. If we head for the most popular rides before it gets too busy, we can maximise our–'

'Dodgems,' Hallie says, already jogging across the grass to the rink where the bumper cars are gleaming.

'Yessss!' I say, running after her.

We get straight on with no queue, joined by a

couple of smug sixth-formers and a pack of Year 8 girls. None of us wants to be a passenger, so we get in a car each, pressing down on the accelerators impatiently while we wait for the ride to start. I'd forgotten how fun the dodgems are, being able to unleash my inner rage without any consequences. Hallie is a savage dodgem driver, as I'd expect. She whoops around the rink, finding the empty spaces so she can use them for epic run-ups. When she hits me, I feel it in every tooth and bone.

After the dodgems we move on to the tower of terror. It's basically like being in a falling elevator.

'Amazing,' Hallie says, when we get off. 'It felt like I was going to fall out because the bar they put over our laps was so loose.'

'And that made you happy?' Naira asks.

Gus's whole face is pink and lit up like Christmas morning. 'Who doesn't love being dropped from a great height?'

'My stomach nearly came out of my throat,

I think.' It's not often that I'm glad I didn't eat more at dinner.

'I actually thought I was going to die.' Colette wobbles on to the grass. 'Something less horrifying next, please.'

The fair is filling up now, Dread Wood pupils flooding through the gates in twos and threes and huge groups. I see Mr Canton trying to chat to one of the fair people by the snack stalls. Probably moved off gate duty because he was too slow. Mr C is talking in his usual way, like everything is interesting and the fair person is his best friend. The fair person looks like he'd rather be dropping from the tower of terror without the safety rail.

There's noise everywhere – music blaring, rides whirring, games beeping and people shouting and laughing. I look around at Gus, Hal, Colette and Naira, and they're all breathless and giddy. Flushed faces and happy smiles. It feels like ages since we were able to enjoy ourselves like this.

'Carousel next,' Gus says. 'Yes, I know it's for little kids, but it's a fairground classic and it would be rude not to ride it.'

'I dibs the rainbow horse,' Colette says, running for the middle of the green where the carousel is glowing like the golden sun at the centre of everything. We all choose our horses and then laugh the whole way around, like we *are* little kids.

The next two hours are a blur. We take goofy selfies, sticking out our slushie-blue tongues and pulling our best gangsta poses. We eat a bunch of food that we wouldn't be allowed to eat anywhere else. We fish for plastic ducks, shoot water at moving targets and throw balls at coconuts. I win a purple bunny plush that I give to Colette. That makes Hallie mad, so we have to waste a ton of tokens trying to win another one for her. We don't leave the game till she has one. Naira wins a giant pink teddy bear for Gus and he says it's the best thing he's ever been given in his life. At some point I stop noticing how shabby and worn out the fair is – now it twinkles like stars.

We don't mention the ghost train. It's like we've silently agreed to avoid it. I catch it in the corner of my vision every now and then, lurking over by the churchyard. Other kids are going on it, coming out laughing and holding their hands over their hearts like they've just had the best jump-scare. But I've had enough of those for a while.

'Look, there's no queue for the Ferris wheel,' Gus yells, and we all leg it over there, bundling into the seats. Me and Colette. Hallie and Naira. Gus and his teddy.

I look around Finches Green as we make the slow climb to the top, our pod swinging and creaking in every breeze. It's Christmas tree bright, and full of happy faces.

'It's magical, isn't it?' Colette says. 'Who'd have thought it?'

'Gus,' I say, and we both snort laugh.

And then suddenly the lights sputter out, the music cuts off, and someone screams.

CHAPTER TWENTY-TWO

LOST IN THE GAME

There's a moment of total darkness and silence. The Ferris wheel has stopped turning, along with everything else in the fairground.

Colette grabs my hand as our eyes adjust to the darkness. 'Is it a power cut?' she whispers.

From where we are, I can see distant lights glowing – the street lights on the main road, some of the windows in the Dread Wood school mansion.

'If it's a power cut, it must be the generators for the fair,' I say. 'I'm sure they'll be back up in a few seconds.'

And they are. As quickly as everything stopped, it starts again. The lights flicker back to life, one by one, but so fast it's like a domino rally. We're jerked in our seat as the Ferris wheel powers up, making us rock violently. I keep one hand gripped on the safety bar and the other in Colette's and close my eyes against the flare of light.

'Angelo,' Colette says, her hand squeezing mine like she wants to break every bone inside. 'Do you see them?'

I open my eyes. Look around. Behind the carousel there's a small raised hut with steps leading up to the door. It has windows on every side so you can see the whole fairground – like a value-range lookout tower. From this height I can see that inside there are control panels covered with switches. Standing over them, looking out of the window and up to where we are, dangling on the Ferris wheel, are two masked figures. My heart, which was flying just a few minutes ago, sinks in my chest like a rock in a pond.

'I see them,' I say.

'Guys,' Naira calls from the pod behind us.

'Yeah,' I call back. 'We know.'

'Surely the fair people will stop them?' Colette gasps, looking around at the stalls and rides. The fair people have gone. Just disappeared. The Latchitts are in control.

'We need to get down,' Hallie says, and I hear her rattling the safety bar. 'This scrutty wheel is too slow.'

'Hallie, sit down,' Naira yells. 'We're hella high and you aren't The Rock. Climbing down isn't an option.'

I turn around. 'Nai's right,' I say. 'We'll be down in a minute. What's the worst they can do before then?'

Even as I'm saying it, I know it's stupid. Even as I'm saying it, I feel how vulnerable we are.

I see the Latchitts wave. I watch them reach down to the control panel. Whatever they're planning, I know it's going to be bad. I look around for anyone who could help – responsible adults, or teachers, or someone I can shout at to stop them, but there's no one there. The teachers must be busy somewhere else. Everyone else is lost in their own conversations. We're the only ones who realise the danger we're all in, and we're stuck up in the air on a rusty metal wheel.

Music starts to play over the speaker system. Loud and rattling, reverberating around the green. Not the pop music from before. The Flinch tune. The Latchitts are playing the Flinch tune. I feel my phone vibrate in my pocket, and I pull it out at the same time Colette grabs hers. They're both lit up and playing the Flinch tune.

'Deleting it didn't work,' I say.

'The Latchitts have control of everyone's phones.' Colette gazes out across the green where every kid is holding a glowing phone and grinning with anticipation.

Instantly, the bees inside me – the ones that I thought were gone – start buzzing and pulsating. I swear every nerve ending in my body is striking up its own microscopic electrical storm.

My first thought is that I need to get off this wheel and do something – although whether that's playing Flinch, or stopping the Latchitts, or something else completely, I don't know. I just know I need to move.

My second thought, as I look around at every other Dread Wood kid apparently feeling the exact same way, is that there's going to be chaos.

'They planned this all along,' Colette says quietly.

'What do we do?' Gus shouts from two pods behind us. I can barely hear him over *Pop Goes the Weasel*.

'We get off this ride and we finish this,' I shout back.

The wheel turns so slowly. Slow enough for us to watch everyone around us absolutely losing

261

it. There are hundreds of kids here, and every one of them is in game mode. They run for the best Flinch spots, shoving each other out of the way, and trampling over people who've had the bad luck to fall or get pushed to the ground. They throw down half-eaten food and barely touched drinks. They ditch the cuddly toys they'd been clutching tightly a moment ago. They even jump from moving rides.

'Where are the teachers, for freak's sake?' Naira shouts. 'Someone needs to stop this.'

The Flinch tune reaches the end of the round opening section – *that's the way the money goes . . .* and then it starts again from the beginning.

'It's on a loop,' Hallie shouts. 'It's not going to end.'

We're halfway back down now. I wonder if we're low enough to jump without getting hurt.

Everywhere, people are screaming, either because they've been flinched, or to make someone else flinch. They're climbing up the sides of the huts so they can launch themselves down on top of people.

'Looks like the no physical contact rule is out,' I say. I put all my strength into pulling the safety bar, hoping I can force it to lift.

'Together,' Colette says. And we pull at the same time. It gives way suddenly and flies upwards. We lunge backwards only just in time to avoid it cracking into our faces.

'You want to jump?' I look at her. We're probably about two metres off the ground now. It's risky as hell, but I'm up for it anyway.

'Let's do it,' she says, turning to the opening on her side of the pod.

I do the same. We don't count down, don't take a breath. We just jump, no hesitation. I hit the ground hard, the wind knocked out of me. My teeth clatter and blood trickles into my mouth. I must have opened up one of the cuts from Wednesday. My messed-up leg screams with pain. I ignore it.

I turn to see Colette bouncing to her feet. She looks rattled, but unhurt.

'Let's go,' she shouts. Everything is so loud. The hydraulic chug and hiss of the rides sounds sinister now, giving me the feeling that they're actually robots about to go fully sentient and kill us all. All around us kids are roaring, screaming, yelling. In fear, in anger, in excitement – I can't even tell which any more. And through it all, the Flinch tune plays on.

Colette and I run to the control hut. I'm ready to face the Latchitts, fight them, destroy them. Whatever it takes. But when we reach the hut, they've gone.

Colette races up the steps. 'They've locked the door. I can't get in.'

'We need to break in,' I gasp, looking around for something I can use to lever the door open. I see Hallie, Naira and Gus running towards us – a few seconds behind because they obviously waited to reach the ground before they exited the wheel.

'What the hell did you think you were doing, jumping out of the ride when you were so high up?' Hallie shouts. 'Have you lost your freaking minds?'

'We needed to hurry,' I say. 'And it didn't seem that high.'

'Guys.' Hallie is red-cheeked and out of breath. 'I'm all for charging head first into stuff, but that was so stupid. You could have broken your necks.'

The thought strikes me, just for a second, that she's right. Hallie is usually the reckless one, so if she thinks it was stupid, then maybe it was. But I push the thought aside – we don't have time.

'We need to get this door open,' I say. 'Stop the music.'

Naira looks around. 'Where are the Latchitts?'

'Gone when we got here,' Colette says, pushing and pulling at the door.

'That's convenient,' Naira mutters.

'Get down!' Gus shouts suddenly, as a bottle flies through the air towards us. I duck just in time for it to miss hitting my head by a couple of centimetres.

'Made you flinch!' some random kid shouts at us. 'Hand over the points.' He holds up his phone to claim the flinches.

'Who the hell even are you?' Hallie shouts at him. 'Get lost.'

'I'll make sure you're eliminated for this,' he yells at us before running off.

'What did you mean, Naira?' Colette asks, coming down the stairs. 'About it being convenient?'

Naira glares at Colette, puts her hands on her hips. She's much taller than Col, so with Colette back on the ground, she's staring down at her. 'It means they only physically attack us when you're not around,' she says.

'They locked me in the library with you,' Colette says. 'Remember?'

'Yeah, but they didn't throw a worm in with us. They just wanted us out of the way so they could get Angelo and Hallie.'

'What are you getting at, Naira?' I ask. 'Because it sounds like you're accusing Colette of something.'

'And to be fair, you've not had a worm thrown at you either, Naira.' Colette stands taller, meeting Naira's eye.

'Yeah, but they did send their killer spiders after her,' Gus says.

I feel myself getting hot with anger. 'Why do you always take Naira's side, Gus?'

He shrugs. 'Why do you always take Colette's?'

'Guys!' Hallie shouts, standing in between us. 'Why are you arguing? Correct me if I'm wrong, but I thought we were all on the same team.'

I watch Naira's face. She's been at this the entire week – making out that Colette's up to god knows what. I've had enough. I'm not backing down this time.

A metal bar suddenly javelins through the air between us and crashes into the steps of the hut.

'Flinch!' some girl screams at us, waving her phone, then runs off without even waiting to collect the points. It's like all rules have been abandoned, and all that matters is playing. I want so badly to chase her and scare her, and for a second I forget about everything other than the need to run into the chaos around me, and become part of it.

'Why do I want to join in so bad?' I say. 'It's like I'm not in control of myself.'

'Same here,' Gus says. 'I know it's wrong but I want it anyway.'

Colette nods. 'The tune plays and I turn into a different person. Like it says in the player's guide – it's like I'm the jack-in-the-box, and someone else is turning the handle, winding me up.' She glances at Naira, but Naira says nothing, just stares at the ground in front of her.

And a sickening thought starts tentacling my brain then. Just at the edges, and so awful that instead of snatching at it, I push it away, at the same time that I feel the itch in my neck that's been bothering me for weeks.

I'm weirdly pleased to see Mr C sprinting towards us.

'Everyone all right?' he asks. He's breathless and sweating. His jumper is torn on one sleeve.

'Gucci,' Hallie says. 'You?'

'We've lost all control,' he says. 'I've never seen behaviour this extreme before. It's like the whole school is on some illegal substance. Maybe someone spiked the pop.'

'It's Flinch,' I say. I point at the hut. 'We need to get inside and stop the music and then we can deal with everyone's phones.'

'Excellent plan. Is it locked?'

'Yeah,' I said. 'Someone doesn't want us getting in.'

Mr Canton nods, gazing at the carnage around him. 'I don't know where the fairground supervisors are – maybe getting reinforcements. The other teachers are dealing with a fist fight behind the fortune-telling tent. We need to get on top of this before someone is seriously hurt. Here's what we'll do. I'm going to go up there . . .' he points to the helter-skelter, 'to get a good view of the whole green so that I can

269

locate all available adults and check the status of the pupils. I'm going to use my trusty whistle to try to get everyone's attention and calm things down. In the meantime, can I ask you guys to put your famous teamwork to good use, and get inside that hut to turn the music off?'

'Of course,' Hallie says. 'We might need to break it open, though.' She does a terrible job of trying to look like she isn't excited at the prospect.

'Whatever you need to do, I'll take full responsibility,' Mr Canton says. 'Quick as you can.' He sprints towards the helter-skelter.

'Can we stop arguing now?' Hallie looks around at us. 'We need to deal with the Latchitts.' Her eyes fall on the metal bar lying in the grass by the hut, and she grins.

I try to squash down the rage inside, pour icy water over the bees. It takes more effort than it should. Hallie picks up the metal bar and climbs the steps to the hut while the rest of us stand frozen. I wonder if they're trying to do the same as me, internally drowning their anger.

The top half of the door has a glass panel. Hallie swings back the bar like a baseball bat and hammers into it. There's a bang so loud that I hear it clearly over the anarchy around us, but the glass doesn't break. She tries again. Once, twice, three times.

A pack of Year 7s have taken over the carousel, standing on the horses, throwing coconuts at anyone who comes close, jabbing at people with hook-ended fishing rods.

I watch a group of kids trying to climb the tower of terror, hanging on one-handed while they use their free hands to shove each other.

Some sixth-formers have ripped the water guns from the shooting gallery and are filling them with any liquid they can find.

I want to join in.

Then I see Mr Canton disappear into the entrance of the helter-skelter, his usually neat jumper soaked with sweat, his trousers covered in dirt, his hair looking like my brother's when he gets out of bed in the morning. For whatever reason, it helps me to see through my fury. I run up the steps to help Hallie.

'Use it like a spear instead,' I say. 'Jab the end near the edge of the glass.'

We hold the bar together and stab it at the window. The glass cracks on the first hit, and smashes completely on the third. I wrap my arm in my hoodie and clear the rest of the glass from the frame, then I climb through the hole and into the hut.

The control panel is about a metre across and has about a hundred different switches. It looks about thirty years old, and the labels that say what the buttons do have rubbed away to nothing. There's a microphone on the desk next to the panel, so I follow the wire that connects it to the rest of the controls, and flick a load of switches until the Flinch tune finally stops.

The sudden quiet is filled with the sharp blast of a PE whistle, and I look through the window to see Mr Canton standing at the top of the helter-skelter, whistle in hand.

'Pupils of Dread Wood High,' he shouts, but everyone just carries on like they haven't heard him. I imagine that jack-in-the-box being wound tighter and tighter. We're all coiled springs, bursting to explode and barely containing ourselves. Something's really wrong here, and it's not going to stop until the app puts an end to it.

Mr Canton blows the whistle again, three shrill shrieks that cut through the noise of the mobs and the rides. No one even looks up.

'It's not enough to turn the Flinch tune off,' I say to the others. 'We need to play the alert for the end of the round.'

'Let me look,' Naira says, jogging up the steps and climbing into the hut next to me. We press buttons, flick switches, turn knobs. Nothing works.

Mr Canton blows his whistle again.

'It's like watching the *Titanic* go down,' Gus says, gazing up at Mr C. 'Lost cause.'

'Don't say that,' Hallie says. 'He'll do it. You know what he always says: if anyone can, Canton ca—'

Her mouth falls open and stays that way, and I look to see what she's seeing.

A masked figure is standing behind Mr Canton. It's someone at least half a metre taller than him and twice as wide, face like an evil jack-in-the-box clown. He raises a gloved hand and waves at us, then we watch in horror as he pulls back both hands and shoves Mr Canton in the back.

CHAPTER TWENTY-THREE

THE WEASEL POPS

Mr Canton tips forward, his eyes wide in shock. The whistle falls from his open mouth, streaking down towards the ground in a flash of silver that alternately glints in the reflected colours of the fairground lights. It must be an eight-metre drop.

For a moment Mr C seems to find his balance, pulling himself back from the edge and wobbling there, arms windmilling, until he gets the better of the momentum pushing him forward. Then

Mr Latchitt shoves him again, and this time there's no slow-motion struggle, no chance to recover himself. Mr Canton tilts forward scarily fast, and he falls.

He plummets face first, arms flailing. We shout, scream, swear. He doesn't. He just falls. In the last fraction of a second before he hits the ground he curls himself into a ball, using his arms to cover his face and head as much as possible. Then he rolls into the earth and lies still.

I jump out of the window, not caring about the shards of glass still stuck in the frame that rip my skin. I take the steps in one leap, land badly, get myself back up and running, aware that the others are with me.

When we reach Mr C, he's lying on his side, his knees bent and his arms still held protectively by his face.

'He looks like he's sleeping,' Colette says.

'Apart from the blood,' Hallie says. Mr C's head is split on one side, and oozing blood into the grass.

I crouch next to him and place my fingers on his neck, just behind his ear to see if he has a pulse. It was only a few months ago that I did this exact same thing, but deep under the school grounds. At least I know what I'm doing better this time. I feel a flutter under my skin.

'He's alive,' I say.

Naira bends down and puts her face close to his. I notice that she's covered in tiny cuts. 'He's breathing too.'

'I'll phone for an ambulance,' Gus says, pulling his phone out of his pocket. He looks at it. Frowns. 'I can't get off the Flinch app to make a call or text or anything. It's stuck on the screen.'

Hallie tries her phone. 'Same for me,' she says.

We all check. None of us can make a call.

'When we downloaded the app we gave them control of our phones,' Colette says. 'They're useless. I'm going to run for help.'

'It's too dangerous.' I shake my head. 'The

Latchitts are here somewhere.' I look around the fairground, which is absolutely trashed. 'Looks like the apocalypse,' I say.

'And none of them have even noticed that their teacher is half dead on the ground,' Naira says. Which is true. Everyone is still in mid-Flinch insanity. People are limping, bleeding, staggering around like they're drunk.

'So what the hell do we do?'

I'm still bent over Mr C, so it makes me jump when he suddenly jolts up, almost headbutting me. 'Whistle. Need my whistle. *Pop goes the weasel*.'

I swear out loud. From surprise and relief and at least ten other feelings that are battering at me.

'Gonna let that one go,' Mr Canton slurs. ''Cos my head hurts.' He slumps back down to the ground, but stays conscious. 'Need my whistle.'

Kids are running across the green holding a weird mix of scavenged weapons. So wrapped up in the game that they don't care who they hurt. I've never seen anything like it.

'This isn't normal,' I say.

'No shiz, Angelo,' Hallie mutters.

'I don't know,' Gus says. 'Most of my family gatherings are like this. Weddings, funerals, first birthdays . . .'

'The ones with cousin Julia?' I ask, and despite everything I let out a snigger.

'I thought we agreed not to discuss that,' Gus says. 'Bro code, man.'

'You're right, sorry,' I say. 'What I mean is, we're missing something. Mr Canton was right – it's like everyone's been drugged or something. They've totally lost control of themselves.'

'It is all quite *Lord of the Flies*,' Naira says.

'Lord of the who, now?' Hallie says.

'It's a book,' Naira says. 'On the Key Stage Three recommended reading list?'

We all just look at her.

Naira sighs. 'Basically a group of kids are alone on an island, and they all completely lose their minds and turn on each other. Which

I don't think is realistic. Sure, you'd get the odd person behaving outrageously, but most would work together, even with their differences. We're proof of that.'

'So the thing that we're missing,' I say. 'The thing that's making everyone go on the rampage like this . . . I've got an idea what it might be, but you're not going to like it.'

We all duck as another missile flies past us and smashes into the helter-skelter.

'We need to move,' Colette says. 'If we stay here, we're going to get hurt, and we need to find somewhere safe to stash Mr C until we can get an ambulance.'

'Changing the subject at a convenient time again,' Naira says. 'Don't you think we need to work out what the hell's going on?'

Colette stands up, clenches her jaw and her fists. 'I just meant taking a few minutes to find somewhere safer to talk. What's your problem with me, Naira?'

Hallie, Gus and I look at each other in alarm.

We need to stop this.

'Colette's right, Nai,' I say. 'We need to move Mr Canton. We can talk about this after.'

'I say we talk about it now.' Naira shoots me the most thunderous look I've ever seen.

Something wet jets through the air and hits my cheek. At first I think someone's spat at me, but then I look up to see the sixth-formers with water pistols legging it towards us, pointing their guns in our direction.

'That makes ninety-seven,' one of them roars, and I realise he means Flinch points. I flinched when the liquid hit my face. 'No one's beating me. I'm the G!' Specks of spit fly from his mouth as he yells.

'You've got something on your face, loser,' Hallie shouts back. He's painted dark brown war stripes on his cheeks. 'Did you use chocolate for that, or your own turds?'

The sixth-former's furious. He opens his mouth to shout back, but something stops him. His body jerks like he's hiccupping. Once. Twice.

Then he starts retching like he's going to vom, his body convulsing and his face so far beyond white that I think it's actually turning grey.

'What's happening?' Colette whispers, taking a step away from him.

'He's gonna blow,' Gus says.

The sixth-former shakes. Opens his mouth again. I can see something inside, something pale and churning. It doesn't look like vomit. It looks like . . .

'Maggots!' Hallie screams, as tiny white worms pour out of the sixth-former's mouth and drop on to the grass where they writhe around blindly, opening and closing their mouths full of tiny, pointed teeth.

'Whoa, whoa, whoa,' Gus shouts. 'What the actual freak is happening right now?'

I look at the worm puke spewing out of the kid's mouth, and the thought I've been pushing away finally forces its way to the front of my mind. 'They're not maggots,' I say, as the sixth-former's mates back away from him and the

282

seething mess at his feet. 'They're the segments of a parasitic worm.'

'You mean he has one inside him?' Naira says, the look of anger on her face replaced with horror.

'Yeah, I think he has. And it's grown so big that it's separated into . . .' I point at the mini worms thrashing around in front of us, 'those.'

He's still barfing the worms – there are hundreds of them – but when he looks up, I see they're crawling out of his nose too. He's choking, struggling to breathe.

'Try to push them out fast,' I shout at him.

I don't know if he hears me, but he keeps gagging and puking, and scraping them out of his mouth with his hands. I want to help, but I have no idea what to do. And then suddenly they stop. One last one dropping from his nostril and plopping down with the rest. The kid gasps, leaning over with his hands on his knees, trying to catch his breath.

'Is it finished?' Colette says. 'How is he even alive after that?'

We all stare at the sixth-former and it's like time stops for a few seconds. Nobody knows what to do or say. But then he calmly picks up the gun that he dropped and shouts, 'Let's get the helter-skelter!' The others roar and cheer, and they all start squirting the helter-skelter behind us with whatever's in their water guns.

'This is insane,' says Hallie. She looks at me. 'Are you saying that the reason some of these previously boring-as-hell kids have suddenly turned into arsonists is because they're being controlled by parasitic worms?'

I bite my lip. Take a second. 'Yeah, that's what I'm saying.'

We stare at the pile of worms, which are wriggling outwards, spreading across the grass.

'We need to move Mr Canton away,' I say.

'Yeah,' Gus whispers. 'The floor is larvae.'

None of us talk as we help Mr Canton up and drag him to a quiet spot at the edge of the fairground between two parked trailers. I have loads to say, but my mind is racing. Replaying what I just saw and trying to understand what it means.

It's only after we've laid Mr C down in the recovery position, propping his head up on Gus's pink teddy and tucking a hoodie over him, that everything really clicks into place in my brain.

'*Pop goes the weasel,*' Mr C sings. '*Pop goes the weasel.*'

We make sure he's as comfortable as possible, then we stand and face each other.

'The weasel went pop, all right,' Gus says.

I nod. 'That must be what the Latchitts meant. The parasites live inside their hosts, feeding on adrenaline and growing bigger and bigger. When they reach a size the host can't contain, they pop. It's the way some parasitic worms reproduce, by making each segment of their body a mini version of themselves.'

'The jack comes out of the box,' says Colette.

'And the baby worms wriggle off to find new

hosts.' Naira looks hella disgusted.

'But he was still a maniac, even after he'd puked all the worms,' Hallie says. 'Surely he should have gone back to normal?'

I rub my face with my hands so hard it hurts. 'I'm thinking that the original worm stays latched on to the brain of the original host.'

'So it can regrow?' Gus gasps.

I nod. 'And the life cycle starts all over again.'

'Oh god.' Colette is bone pale. 'Flinch just speeds everything up. It makes the hosts get hundreds of adrenaline rushes.'

'The worms grow faster. And . . . oh god.' Naira pushes her hair back. Takes a deep breath. I'm sure she's thinking what I'm thinking.

'There's something we need to face up to,' I say, looking around at the others. I don't think they know. I think, just like I did earlier, they've pushed the idea away because it's too awful to think about.

'What is it?' Colette asks.

I put my hand to the back of my neck – the

place I've been having that itch for weeks now. And I feel it – the thing I was desperately hoping not to feel. There's something moving under my skin.

'I think we're all infected.'

CHAPTER TWENTY-FOUR

THE BRUTAL TRUTH

'No way,' Gus says. He looks like he's going to be sick.

'Angelo's right,' Naira says. 'Think about it. We've already admitted that we've not been acting like ourselves lately. We've been snappy, stroppy . . .'

'Quick to lose our tempers with each other,' I say. 'And to rush into dangerous situations without thinking about the consequences.' I let that sink in for a second. 'And remember when we talked about feeling like there was something buzzing inside our bodies?'

'Yeah, but that's just a thing you say.' Colette's face is new-snow white. 'I didn't mean there was an actual living thing inside me.'

'But it adds up,' Naira says. 'Anyone else had an itch?'

'On the back of my neck.' I turn around and point to where I felt the movement. 'Put your hands here. You can feel it.'

Naira puts her fingertips firmly on my skin, then moves them to the back of her own neck. 'There's something there. And on mine too.' She turns to Gus. 'Let me check you.'

'Er, no,' Gus says. 'Absolutely not.'

'Check me.' Colette turns and lifts her hair up off her neck. 'I've had an itch.'

I don't even need to touch her. I see a small lump rise and fall in her neck, moving under the skin like it has a mind of its own. I put my hand to it and feel it push back against me.

'You have one,' I say.

Colette bites her lip and turns her face away. I can see she's trying really hard not to cry. Naira crouches down, puts her head in her hands. I leave them to their thoughts. We all need to find a way to deal with this.

'The itch thing makes sense,' Hallie says. 'Remember how Michelle was tearing at her skin? But I don't have one. At least I don't think I do.'

'You want me to check?' I say.

'Yeah.' She turns around. 'I need to know.'

I feel the part of Hallie's neck where the parasite should be, just beneath the skin. But there's nothing there. No lumps, no movement. I take my hand away, flex my fingers, and try again. Nothing.

'I don't think you have one, Hal,' I say. 'I don't feel or see anything.'

'That can't be right.' Naira stands up. 'Let me check.' She examines Hallie's neck, poking at it so hard that I think she might break the skin. 'You're right, Angelo,' she says at last.

'Hallie's clear.'

'Thinking about it, there have been a couple of times recently when Hallie's been the sensible one. She recovered much quicker than I did after the toilet incident. She was so calm, covering for me when I couldn't get myself together. I remember thinking it was weird that she wasn't still charging around like a vengeful bull. No offence, Hal. And she was angry at us for jumping out of the Ferris wheel earlier.'

'OK, firstly, offence taken, Angelo,' Hallie says. 'Secondly, quit stabbing me with your witch finger, Naira. And thirdly, while I am totally stoked that I don't have a brain-biting worm inside me, how can that be? Am I not good enough to be worm fodder?'

Assuming that basically every Dread Wood kid at the fair is infected with a parasite, it does seem strange that Hallie isn't. But her chicken is. I think back to what the Latchitts said in the Dread Wood. I turn to Gus. 'We need to check you, man. I know it's grim, but I have a theory, and knowing whether or not you have a worm is going to help me see if I'm right.'

'God, fine,' Gus huffs. 'But if you find one, I can't promise I'm not going to totally lose my shiz.'

Both Naira and I check the back of his neck, and yeah, there it is. Like a cartoon mouse under a cartoon rug. A small lump moving around, making its home under Gus's skin.

'Don't freak out,' Naira says.

'You telling me not to freak out suggests that you're about to tell me something that will make me freak out.' Gus turns to face us again. 'Hit me with it. Can't promise I won't vom, but I'll try not to get it on your shoes.'

Naira shrugs. 'You have a worm wrapped around your spine. I can see it wiggling about.'

Gus turns and vomits on to the grass. There's a lot of pink in it from the candy floss he stuffed in his face earlier. Mostly the pink puke misses us. I try to ignore the bit of splashback that spatters on to my trousers.

'Maybe try to think of it as a friend, rather than a parasite?' I say.

Gus stands straight and wipes his mouth with a tissue Colette hands to him. He has tears streaming down his cheeks and he's borderline hyperventilating.

'Take deep breaths, Gus,' Hallie says, putting her hand on his chest. 'Breathe with me. In through the nose. Out through the worm.'

Gus splutters out a snort, and practically screams with laughter. Of course that makes the rest of us start laughing too. Things are so bad. What else can we do?

'You know things have got really weird when Hallie becomes the funny one,' Gus says when he's calmed down a bit. 'Truly it is the miracle we never knew we needed.'

'Oi.' Hallie whacks him in the arm. 'I'm funny, like, all the time.'

Gus makes a face. 'Sure you are, Hal.'

'Rude. I'm going to put that down to the fact you're being controlled by a worm.'

293

'Oh god, the worm.' Gus rubs his face so hard he leaves finger marks. 'The freaking worm.'

'I have a question,' Naira says. 'If we have worms the same as everyone else, why aren't we acting the same way they all are?' She points at the fairground carnage. 'I mean, I know we all want to, but we're stopping ourselves.'

'I think I know,' Colette says. 'The brain-biters feed on adrenaline, right? They probably don't care how they get it, as long as when they're awake they're feeding.'

'So everyone here is playing Flinch to get that rush . . .' Hallie says.

'But we're getting that rush whether we're playing or not,' Colette says. 'We have far worse things to be scared of than a bunch of hyped-up teenagers throwing soda cups. So now that we know we shouldn't play Flinch, we can resist it, as long as our worms are still getting their adrenaline.'

'Which they are because, though I know I hide it well, I'm scared to death right now,' Gus says.

'How am I supposed to get my head around the fact that I have a giant worm wrapped around my spine?'

'You could name your worm,' Colette says, putting her arm around him.

'I *do* like to name things,' Gus sniffs.

Colette smiles at him. 'You can name mine too, if you like.'

Gus blows his nose. 'That means a lot, thank you. How about Nigel?'

We're interrupted by what sounds like a small explosion somewhere in the fairground. Even though the Flinch tune has stopped playing, the situation hasn't improved any. It's not going to until the alert plays to end the round.

'What was your theory, Angelo?' Naira asks. 'And is it going to help us sort this mess out?'

'So,' I say. 'Everyone's infected except for Hal. Hallie was there both times the Latchitts set worms on us. The whole time we thought they were trying to infect all of us, but they were only trying to infect Hallie because they knew she was worm free.'

'How did they know?' Hallie asks.

'Remember Mrs Latchitt said they planted seeds ages ago? Whenever she says anything, there's usually a double meaning. I think they planted worms in the school chickens. The chickens whose eggs and meat were used in the school dining hall . . .'

'Oh man, the chicken burgers,' Gus says.

Naira nods. 'And Hallie's veggie, so she didn't eat anything contaminated.'

'Exactly.'

'That makes sense, Angelo,' Colette says. 'But it doesn't help us to fix things.'

'No, it doesn't,' I say. 'But we know that the Latchitts train their creatures using nursery rhymes, right? That's what they did with the spiders.'

'They used the song to stop them from attacking,' Hallie says.

'So what if they're using the tune to control the worms, but in a different way?' I say.

Gus gasps. 'They've been using the Flinch tune to wake the worms up so they can eat.'

'They hear the tune, wake up and put pressure on our brains so that we run around like crazy people, getting pumped up on adrenaline and scaring the shiz out of everyone else,' Colette says.

I nod. 'Like a dinner bell. Remember it was when the Flinch app played in Hal's garden that Michelle totally lost it?'

'And the last part of the tune tells the worms to go back to sleep,' says Naira. 'That's what we need to do – play the last part of the song to shut the worms down.'

'How, though?' Colette says. 'We can't control everybody's phones, and even if we could work out how to play something over the fair's loudspeakers, we don't have a recording of it and we can't access YouTube. I don't think it will work if we sing it, because we've all been singing it constantly for weeks when it's been stuck in our heads. It only works when the app plays it.'

'Don't you think it's strange that the Latchitts haven't come after us at the fair?' I say. 'We know they're here, controlling the chaos, but they haven't approached us.'

'They're the only ones with the stupid Flinch tune,' Hallie groans. 'They know we'll have to go looking for them.'

'Right,' I say. 'And as they want us to find them, I have a good idea where they're going to be.'

Naira swears, which is a good indication of how wrecked we are. 'The ghost train.'

CHAPTER TWENTY-FIVE

GHOST TRAIN

Getting to the other side of the green should be the easiest of easy things.

But right now it's like heading out to scavenge for tinned goods at the end of the world. There are at least a hundred obstacles between us and the ghost train.

We check that Mr Canton is as OK as he can be before we leave. He's cuddling two plush bunnies and humming to himself, so not brilliant, but could be worse.

'We'll be back soon, sir,' I say. 'Just stay right

299

there and try not to draw attention to yourself.'

'I shall remain on guard and protect these rabbits with my life,' Mr C says. 'No caps will be popped on my watch, doggs.'

'I'm going to let that slide because you have a head injury,' Hallie says. 'But when all this is over we really need to discuss your use of street slang.'

'Shh,' says Mr C, closing his eyes. 'The rabbits are trying to sleep.'

'I feel bad leaving him,' Colette says, as we edge back towards the fairground, keeping our backs to the trailers and peering around the corner.

'The only other option is for us to split up,' says Naira. 'Some of us stay with him and the rest go to the ghost train. But if we're going to face the Latchitts, we need to be together to have a chance of . . .'

She tails off without finishing her sentence, but she doesn't need to. We all know how dangerous the Latchitts are, and what they're capable of. What she was going to say is that we need to be together to have a chance of making it out alive.

'The good thing is that it's going to be totally easy to stay calm,' Gus says. 'You know, so our worms don't pop.'

'Yeah, I'm feeling super calm right now,' Colette says. 'Like I'm strolling along a tropical beach, soft, frothy waves lapping over my feet. Unicorns are grazing, kittens are skipping and the trees are covered in twinkly lights. Ooh, and there are those cute swimming pigs I've seen on TV.'

The fairground is in a worse state than when we left it, and it was shocking then. The ground is covered in debris. Bits of wood and metal, smashed glass, items stolen from stalls and then abandoned. Someone has made a barricade out of arcade machines from the marquee, and there's a group of kids sheltering behind them and taking pop shots with air guns at anyone who gets too close. In between the trash, there are puddles of baby brain-biting worms, twisting and thrashing in angry waves. There's a strong smell of burning, and when I look up I see swirls of black smoke muffling the glow of the lights. Something's clearly on fire.

'This what you were expecting from the fair, Gus?' I say.

'The fair is her own mistress. She follows not the rules of man. It's her unpredictability that makes her so irresistible.' Gus looks left and right like he's waiting for a gap in the traffic so he can cross the road safely.

'Gus, you're never going to get a girlfriend if you keep talking like that,' Naira snorts.

'There's only room for one lady in my life anyway,' Gus says.

'So your parasite identifies as female?' says Hallie.

We all start laughing again. 'Good one, Hal,' Naira snorts.

'She knows I meant the fair, right?' Gus says. 'I don't even know what's happening right now.'

'Right now looks like a good time to run,' Colette says. 'To the burger stand, yeah?'

'Yeah,' I say. 'Let's go.'

We stick to the edges of the fairground as much as possible. It's darker here, in the places where the lights don't quite reach. It means we can use the shadows for cover, but it also means we get surprised by some of the less crazed flinchers lurking in the gloom. We all flinch five or six times, which shouldn't matter considering everything else that's going on, but I still find myself getting annoyed. I don't even know if it's because the worm is making me angry, or if I'm just stupidly competitive.

'What did we even do before Flinch happened?' I say.

'Ate crisps and watched funny stuff on the internet,' Gus says.

'Let's go back to that once this is all over.' Naira's a metre ahead of us and she puts a hand up to tell us to stop moving. A group of Year 10 kids run past waving shafts of wood that are burning at the ends.

'Literally a mob with flaming torches,' Colette says. 'Such a cliché.'

'Maybe we should sing to keep ourselves calm,' Naira says.

'No!' the rest of us shout at the same time, and it helps a bit because it makes us laugh.

Once the angry mob is safely past and clambering aboard the swinging pirate ship, we carry on.

The ghost train is set back from the other rides, with its back to the churchyard. Tombstones rise up behind it, gleaming dull grey in the weak light that makes it that far from the rest of the fair.

'It's almost like they put it here on purpose,' Hallie whispers.

The ghost train itself is the deadest thing around, except for the graves obviously. The carts are empty and still on their rails. The lights are out. There are no sounds escaping from its closed doors.

'So what's the plan?' Colette whispers. We're hiding behind a betting game that's mostly avoided being ransacked like the rest of the fair. Usually its plastic horses would be moving mechanically over an astro-turf track, while spectators cheer them on like the outcome hasn't already been decided by the old-fashioned version of algorithms. But the power cable's been pulled out, and it's stuck mid-race. It gives us enough cover that if anyone is looking out from the ghost train, they won't be able to see us.

'Do we even have a plan?' Gus asks. 'I thought we were just running in, commando style, all guns blazing?'

'I thought we were going for stealth,' Naira says. 'Find a back-door fire exit. Keep the element of surprise.'

'So what's it gonna be?' Hallie says. 'Strength or stealth?'

'We play it like we'd play Flinch,' I say. 'Try to throw them off. Make them think we're doing one thing when we're really doing another.'

'How, exactly, when they know we're coming? They've been about ten steps ahead of us the whole time, just like before,' Naira says.

'They're expecting us to come, but they're also expecting us to be . . . not ourselves,' I say.

'You mean they're expecting us to be raging like Kylo Ren on a hormonal day,' Gus says.

'Exactly. They'll expect us to have no control. To not trust each other. To be fighting. Let's use that.'

'There's something else we can use too,' Naira says. 'I think there's a reason they keep wearing those masks, and it isn't just to creep us out. The masks protect their faces from the brain-biters – they cover all the holes. So just follow my lead, all right?'

'It's not much of a plan,' Colette says. 'No offence.'

'But it's all we have, so we'll give it everything we've got.' Gus does a quiet whoop. 'May the goddess of the fair bless us with the favour of good fortune.' He gazes towards the golden carousel. 'Amen.'

'Amen,' I say, because it feels better than anything else I can think of.

'Amen,' Colette says, hugging Gus, then Hallie, then Naira.

'This goes against everything I believe in, but whatever,' Hallie says. 'Amen.'

'So lame,' Naira mutters.

'Say it, Naira, or the goddess will be displeased, and if the Latchitts kill and eat us, it will be all your fault,' Gus says. 'Say it.'

'Cannibalism again?' Naira raises an eyebrow. 'I'll amen to that. Now let's go. And try not to go pop.' She stands and starts walking towards the ghost train. The plan is on.

'This is it,' I say to the others. 'Sorry in advance for the horrid stuff I'm going to say.'

'Don't worry about it.' Hallie smiles. 'I'm more worried about what Nai's going to come out with. She's the best at being mean.'

I grin, then I stand up too. 'Wait up,' I shout

after Naira. 'It's so annoying when you storm off ahead.' I jog to catch up. 'It's like you think you're in charge.'

'Pretty sure she *is* in charge, mate,' Gus says, joining us as we march across the grass.

Colette comes from behind to walk next to me. 'When did we decide that Naira is the leader? I don't remember agreeing to that.'

'No offence, but if you want to leave this fairground alive, then you should be doing exactly what I say.' Naira does her fiercest glare. 'And let's not forget that it's *your* grandparents who caused this trash-fire.'

Oof – Hallie was right. Straight in with the low blows.

'It's not Col's fault her grandparents are evil,' I say.

We've reached the ghost train now, so we stop and look up at it.

'Angelo takes Colette's side *again*,' Hallie says. 'Shocker.'

'What's that supposed to mean?' Colette says.

'It means,' Naira sighs, 'that you always jump to her defence, even when it's blindingly obvious that Colette is totally . . .'

'. . . sussy,' Gus finishes. 'For all we know, she's been in on the Latchitts' plan from the start.'

I shove Gus in the shoulder, hard enough to look real but not so hard I hurt him. 'Take that back.'

'Get your hands off him.' Hallie pushes me away, much harder, because, you know, it's Hallie. 'He's only saying what the rest of us have been thinking.'

'Touch Angelo like that again, and I'll punch you.' Colette steps towards Hallie, and I'm shocked by how aggressive she looks.

'Just try it.' Naira steps up too. 'I've been itching for an excuse to smash that smug look off your irritating pixie face.'

I'm not sure who throws the first punch because I'm trying not to laugh out loud about 'pixie face', but we somehow end up in a group brawl. Everyone hitting everyone else. All of us rolling around on the ground like a pack of rabid wolves. After a long couple of minutes, and after cracking me around the jaw way harder than is necessary, Naira breaks away from the rest of us and stands up, trying to catch her breath.

'This is a waste of time,' she says. 'Let's go back to the fair and leave these two pathetic losers to go it alone. They won't last long. Come on Hal. Gus.'

Hallie and Gus stand up too, and the three of them jog off back towards the lights of the fairground.

I push myself off the floor and reach down to help Colette up. 'We don't need them,' I say.

Colette nods and we turn towards the ghost train again.

'Ready for this?' I ask.

'Ready,' she says.

As we walk towards the entrance of the ride, I can hear the sounds of every Dread Wood kid unravelling back on the main part of the fairground. I almost prefer it to the deathly quiet around the ghost train.

We climb the steps to where the carts are lined up, waiting to push through the ghost train doors. The double doors are black, with badly painted words written all over them in a classic horror font: 'BEWARE', 'TERROR AHEAD', 'ENTER AT OWN RISK'. All dripping blood and leering skulls.

'I think they're going for a forbidding vibe,' Colette snorts.

She's standing there, smudged glasses, tangled hair and filthy clothes, but she doesn't look afraid. When this started, back in November, she was freaked out. Horrified at the thought of what her grandparents were doing. She's one of the sweetest people I've ever known, and the fact that people had been hurt, and chickens and a pig had been killed in her name, must have been hard to swallow. And even though it all revolved around her, she hadn't actually been there for any of it. She had to hear about it from us, through second-hand stories describing things that must have been almost impossible to imagine. Anyone would find that hard to deal with. Now her totally messed-up grandparents are back for more. And she's stepping up to face them.

I remember her saying that her mum taught her to do whatever it takes to survive, and I think her mum would be proud right now. I want to tell her how proud *I* am of her right now, but I can't say it out loud. Instead I grin at her like an idiot. Squeeze her elbow like a weirdo. I think she gets the message, though. She squeezes mine back.

We step on to the tracks, and push open the doors. Inside it's pitch-black, and the less dark darkness from outside that seeps in barely makes a dent. I literally can't see anything after the point the dim light stretches to – about a metre in front of us. Colette and I grab each other's hands for safety – the last thing we want is to get separated – and take a step forward into god knows what. The doors swing shut behind us.

'We should prop them open,' she says. But when we turn to push through them again, they're already locked.

I swear out loud. 'What a freaking stupid error – I can't believe I let them close so easily.'

'Maybe they're one way only,' Colette says. 'Whatever, we can't do anything about it now. Let's just carry on.'

There are many different versions of the dark, and I'm not scared of most of them. Never have been. I find it hard to understand when Raph needs me to get up and turn on every light in the flat if he needs to pee in the night. Night-time in the city is never really dark. When you're in your home, there's always the glow of street lights and headlights through your window, and the reassuring shine from others nearby that tell you you're not the only person in the country who's awake. Outside you have all those things, plus the silver tinge of light from the moon and stars. The only things that are likely to sneak up on you are foxes and cats, and I always feel lucky when I see one of those. But this dark, trapped inside a box made from metal and plastic, sealed into a space that's been made to keep the light out, is a whole different thing. I don't know where I'm placing my feet. The ground could be solid, or it could open up beneath me. There could be anything up ahead, either side, above me, or below me. I have no clue. I'm blind and confined, and I hate it.

But we walk forward anyway, trying to feel our way along the cart tracks with our feet. We know they'll lead us through and out the other side, so if we keep them underneath us, we can't get lost.

For a few seconds there's no sound except for the creak of our footsteps, but the quiet is broken by a sudden flash of green light and a witchy cackle straight out of *The Wizard of Oz*. I jump from the suddenness, not because it's scary. Then I curse myself because I really don't want my worm to max out and explode. There's another moment of darkness, then the green light strobes on and off, over and over again. The creepy laughter bounces from corner to corner, getting louder and more crazed. A shadow rushes across our path, so fast I can't make out what it is.

'You saw that, right?' Colette says.

'Yeah. Just a light display, not an actual person,' I say, and squeeze her hand. 'Standard ghost train stuff.' We keep walking.

A cold breeze comes at us out of nowhere, along with a hissing sound and a few puffs of dry ice.

'Smells like a primary school disco,' Colette says.

'You went to those?' I snort.

'They were fun. Of course you were way too cool to go to school discos, even in Year 4.' I can practically hear her rolling her eyes.

'I'm glad you realise that,' I say with a smile.

A shrill scream interrupts our chat, and something brushes past our backs. I jump again, which is so annoying because I'm willing myself to stay calm.

'Punk-ass bees,' I say. Because no matter how hard I try, I can't stop them.

'Mine too,' Colette says.

There's another teen slasher scream. My heart pounds.

'I didn't realise Gus was in here with us,' I say, and Colette and I crack up laughing. I feel a movement behind us and brace myself for a scratch on my shoulder or scuttle across my neck.

But Colette lets go of my hand and turns around. 'Sick of all of this,' she says, reaching out and grabbing at the shadow that's stalking us. She catches it in her hands, lets out a roar and yanks it hard. There's a splintering sound, a shower of dust, and she turns back to me holding a plastic witch with broken wires hanging off it where she's pulled it off the ceiling.

'All right, She-Hulk,' I say. I'm so impressed, though.

'You were right,' she says, casually dropping the witch on the floor and stomping on it. 'Pound-shop Halloween junk. Let's go to the next room.'

She takes my hand again, and pushes open the door in front of us. Beyond it there's nothing to see except darkness, but she leads me through without hesitating. 'Whatever's waiting for us in here, bring it on.'

CHAPTER TWENTY-SIX

JACK OUT THE BOX

The door closes behind us, shutting out the flashing green and the broken body of the witch. We take a few steps forward, still trying to keep our feet on the tracks. I can feel my hand sweating, and even with everything that's going on, I find a few seconds to be embarrassed.

Suddenly the room is flooded with bright white light. It's almost painful after the pitch-black, and I automatically raise my free hand to shield my eyes. All I can see is glare, so I squeeze them shut for a moment. When I open them, I get a glimpse of white walls, dripping with blood, and a figure standing in the corner. Then we're plunged into darkness again. The darkness lasts for five of my quickened breaths, and then the blinding-white glare returns. I try to force my eyes to stay open, but apparently I have barely any control over my own body right now, because the lids fly down again. Just for a second. When they flick up again, I see the stark walls, the dripping blood. The figure has disappeared. I notice there's something written on the walls in red, over and over again.

'Don't blink,' Colette reads out in a whisper.

The lights go out again.

After seven heartbeats, they come back on. I blink. When my eyes open I see the figure has returned and is a step closer to us than it was before. It looks like one of those creepy Victorian-type dolls with a china face and painted-on features. Its clothes are old-fashioned, and dirty and tattered.

The lights go out again.

'This one's a head-wrecker,' I say, bracing myself for the next blast of white. When it comes, the figure has gone.

'Sure is,' Colette says, as the room goes black. 'They should have opened with this one.'

There's a longer wait for the lights to come on this time. I'm just starting to think they're not going to, when white sears into my eyeballs again. Of course I blink. My eyes open to find the doll another step closer. I *know* it's on some kind of mechanism and not actually possessed by a demon, but it's very realistic.

Darkness covers us again, like an iron blanket. 'Next time the lights come on, she'll be gone,' I say. 'We run for the door. Get out of here.'

'Yeah,' Colette says. 'I hate this room.'

I tense my muscles, ready to run the moment I can see where we're going.

The light burns on, but as my eyes open, all

I can see is the face of the doll, centimetres from mine.

Colette screams.

I push past the doll and run to the door, pulling Colette with me. I don't look back as I crash through into the next room.

The first thing that hits me is the stink. It's decay and burnt hair and leftover food covered in flies. It takes me back to the spider nest. I gag, and then try to breathe through my mouth.

This room is dark, but has enough light for shadows to form, and for every blurred shape and outline to look like something sinister. We walk towards where the exit must be. I try not to think about the walls closing in on us, or what could be hiding in those shadows.

'What the freak was that?' Colette says, whipping her head around. 'Something touched the back of my neck.'

There's nothing there. So we keep moving.

Then something drops on to my head from

above. It's small and light, but definitely not my imagination. I let go of Colette's hand and frantically swipe at my head until I'm sure there isn't a creature crawling through my hair.

'What happened?' Colette says.

'I don't know,' I say, taking her hand again. 'It's fine. Let's keep going.'

The second we start moving, the room comes alive with blood-red strobe lights, and dark shapes emerge from every nook and shadow.

'Spiders,' Colette gasps.

I look around at the hairy legs and gleaming clusters of eyes. 'Hell, no,' I say. And I run for the door again, batting away anything that lowers itself into my path. I know they're fake, but they look enough like the ones we faced to freak me out.

As we fall into the next room, I realise the cart tracks have stopped so we have no path to follow. It's dimly lit, full of mirrors, but other than that seems empty.

'This can't be good,' Colette says. We start weaving in and out of the mirror maze, carefully trying to find a way through. Then a horribly familiar tune starts to play.

'Flinch,' I say. But it's not through our phones, or the speakers. It's coming from somewhere in the maze. 'They're trying to make us totally lose it. They must be close.'

'This is it then,' Colette whispers.

She's not smiling any more. Her jaw is clenched, and she looks focused. Determined. I feel like she's tapping into that iron streak we know she has. I remember how Gus described her once: ninety per cent Disney princess, ten per cent world's most deadly assassin. Right now she looks one hundred per cent bad-ass. We step forward into the maze.

Every mirror seems to reflect leering faces and tiny movements that I spin around to see but can never quite catch. Another head-wrecker. I focus on not flinching. As we turn what feels like the fiftieth corner, we find the source of the tune. There's a metal cube on the floor, rusty and dented, and covered in pictures of clowns. It has a handle on one side, which is rotating on its own as the music plays.

We stop and look down at it.

'We're obviously not going to touch it, right?' I say.

'Right,' Colette says. 'When a creepy music box turns up in a movie and someone picks it up or bends down for a closer look, they always get killed. Let's keep as far away as possible and leave it alone.'

We walk towards the box, keeping as close to the mirrors either side as we can, side-stepping past it like it's a ticking bomb. We're almost past when the handle stops turning and the music stops. We freeze, look at each other, waiting for something to happen. And then the lid of the box springs open, releasing the creepiest jack-in-the-box clown I've ever seen, its white painted face grinning at us with razor-blade teeth as it bounces on its spring.

And the mirrors around us fill with life-size versions of the same clown face. The Latchitts smile at us from every direction.

CHAPTER TWENTY-SEVEN

BETRAYAL

Colette lets go of my hand and grips my wrist instead, so hard it almost hurts. 'Finally,' she says. 'I've brought a present for you, Grandparents.'

I look at her face, trying to work out what she means. Her eyes are cold and her mouth is twisted into a nasty grin.

'We hoped you would come, sweetling.' About twenty Mrs Latchitts clap their hands from the maze of mirrors. 'We've been yearning for you for such a long time, and here you are at last, our own precious girl.'

'Why didn't you come alone?' Mr Latchitt's voice booms from everywhere and nowhere. I can't pin down where they're hiding.

'He follows me like a puppy, Grandfather,' Colette says.

I meet her eyes and I know my hurt feelings are showing on my face.

She raises an eyebrow. 'And then I figured, why not bring him to you. I know how much you hate him, and I thought he might be useful for testing your creations on.'

'A wily fox to put in the pot,' Mrs Latchitt giggles. 'I can think of many uses for him.'

'So will you come with us now?' Mr Latchitt says. 'Will you join our family? There's someone desperate to meet you.'

Colette looks around at all the mirror images of her grandparents. 'There's someone else?'

'Oh yes, my dearest one,' Mrs Latchitt says. 'Our little family of three has been toiling away for years to bring you here. We'll be together, the four of us, as we should be.'

Colette smiles. 'Who is the other member of our family, Grandmother?'

I'm properly shaken by this news, but if Colette is too then she's hiding it well.

Mrs Latchitt laughs and claps. 'It's a surprise, my duckling. A wonderful, magical surprise. We won't spoil it now. We must hurry away and you will soon know.'

'But where will we go?' Colette says. I can't believe she's the same girl I've spent the last few months talking and laughing with. The person I trusted above everyone else.

'Somewhere we can continue our work without interference,' Mr Latchitt says. 'We have lots of exciting things to show you.'

'Will we not be in trouble?' Colette looks worried for a moment. 'The fairground is destroyed and the children are not in their right minds.' It's like she learned to speak Latchitt.

'There will be no trouble for us, sweetling,' Mrs Latchitt says. 'We have a very special helper with blackbirds in many pies.'

'I'm afraid I don't understand,' Colette says.

'Let my first lesson to you be this,' Mr Latchitt says. 'You only need two things in order to have control over people: money and information.'

'Secret squirrels,' Mrs Latchitt says with a smile. 'If you know their secrets and you buy them treats, they'll do whatever you say.'

My mind is racing, trying to piece everything together. There's a third player. A helper. Someone with money and power. Someone who can find out people's secrets. I want to ask questions but I'm afraid to speak.

'Is that why the fair people left?' Colette asks. 'Because you told them to?'

Mr Latchitt grins. 'As I said, they like money, and they have secrets they don't want the world to know. Everyone does.'

Colette nods. 'You're so clever, Grandfather. But how far does your power stretch? Surely there are those that you can't control?'

'You refer to the police?' Mr Latchitt laughs.

'Blackbirds in pies,' Mrs Latchitt sings. 'Blackbirds in pies. Now we must hurry away. Are you ready, dearest one?'

Colette nods. 'I am. But first may I see your faces? The only times I looked at you in school, you were strangers to me. I want to look at you, knowing that you're my grandparents.'

There's a pause as the Latchitts make the decision, and then they remove their masks. They look the same as they did in November. Even after everything that's happened and all the months that have passed, it's like nothing has changed. Then they step out from where they're hiding – Mrs Latchitt in front and to the right of us, Mr Latchitt to the left.

Colette's grip tightens on my wrist. Maybe I should be trying to fight it, to twist away from her, but there's so much going on in my head that I can't seem to take action.

'Sweetling.' Mrs Latchitt drops her mask on the floor and holds her arms open to Colette.

Mr Latchitt moves towards us, the menace on

329

his face making him look even creepier than he did in the mask.

Colette pulls me roughly so that I'm closer to her. My heart is thudding, my mouth dry, every nerve ending in my body tingling like I'm being stung. I know we had a plan. I know that plan was to pretend. But this betrayal feels so real, and so wrong, and it's like my heart is going to break and my worm is going to pop.

I think back to playing Flinch in the Dread Wood, when I first felt the itch in my neck and I imagined my body exploding into the trees. I would have preferred that than for things to end here, in this place, with these people.

And then two sets of hands appear behind Mrs Latchitt. I see them in the mirrors before I see them in real life. Naira and Hallie barrel into her, grabbing her arms and pinning her against one of the mirrors. Mrs Latchitt screams and fights against them. Hal and Naira struggle to hold her. I remember how strong she is for someone so tiny – heaving the lid of the well in her garden like it weighed nothing. Mr Latchitt growls and starts bounding towards them, but then Gus steps out next to Naira, holding a paper soda cup.

'I wouldn't do that, if I were you,' he says, reaching into the cup and pulling out a tiny brain-biter between the tips of his fingers. He dangles it by Mrs Latchitt's face. Both the Latchitts freeze, and stare at him. 'Give us the tune to end the game.'

'There's no use in hopping along now, little bunnies,' Mrs Latchitt says. 'We've already smoked out your burrow.'

'You want the worm in your wife's ear?' Naira says. 'Or her mouth?'

'Because we'll do it,' Hallie says.

'I will end you,' Mr Latchitt roars, spit flying from his mouth.

'Give us the tune,' Gus says again.

Colette lets go of my arm. 'Now,' she says, staring at Mrs Latchitt. 'This needs to stop.'

I look across at Colette's face. Still determined,

but it's lost that awful cold look it had a few moments ago. She glances back at me and gives me a nod and a half-smile. Her eyes are kind. I almost cry with relief.

'Sweetling?' Mrs Latchitt tilts her head and stares at Colette. 'They tarnished our treasure and they must be punished.'

'No,' Colette says. 'Give us the last part of the Flinch tune.'

'Treasure.' Mrs Latchitt looks confused now. 'Your mind has been poisoned by the wily fox.'

'I'm not your treasure,' Colette says. 'I'm not *your* anything. Give us the final line of the tune or get brain-bitten by your own parasite.'

'Traitor,' Mrs Latchitt hisses. Then she starts laughing. Mr Latchitt too.

'Do I have vomit on my face or something?' Gus says, still holding the worm. 'What's so funny?'

My heart sinks. For all our planning, they still know something we don't know.

'We don't have it,' Mr Latchitt says. 'We have

no intention of stopping the game. Why would we bring it?'

'You're lying,' Naira says.

'We're not.' Mrs Latchitt beams like she's just won the goddamn lottery. 'The game will continue until everyone's popped, over and over again. Pop, pop, pop!'

'I don't think they're lying,' Hallie says.

'So what happens next?' I say. 'Looks like we have a deadlock.'

'We are prepared to make a deal, wily fox,' Mrs Latchitt says. 'If Colette will come with us, and promises to remain at our side, we will tell you how to send the famished ones back to sleep.'

'No,' I say. 'Colette's not going with you.'

'And even if she did, you wouldn't tell us,' Naira says. 'I mean, do you think we're completely stupid?'

Colette takes a step towards Mrs Latchitt. 'Do you promise?' she says. 'That if I come with you, you'll stop the game?'

'Step back, Colette,' Hallie says. 'You're going nowhere.'

'But it might be the only way we can stop the worms,' Colette says.

Mrs Latchitt smiles. 'My little famished ones. Only we know how to shake them awake and rock them gently back to sleep. You need us, sweetling.'

Colette looks between Mr and Mrs Latchitt, and Naira, Gus, Hallie and me.

'Don't do it, Col,' Gus says, moving the worm closer to Mrs Latchitt's ear.

I look at it writhing around, teeth gnashing, and something snags at my brain. It has a mouth. It has teeth. But it doesn't have a nose, eyes or ears. So how can it hear? How does the tune wake it up? Colette is biting her lip and I can see that she's deciding to go with the Latchitts.

'Don't even think about it, Colette,' Naira says. 'We'll find another way.'

I will my mind to work faster. Mrs Latchitt said they shake the worms awake and rock them to sleep. They're controlled through movement, not sound. And that's it – the connection I've been reaching for. They're controlled through *movement*, not sound. Frequencies and vibrations. And Michelle's worm let go and died when the vet used an electric razor on her neck. It must have been the buzz of the razor that finished it. We don't need the tune, we just need to create the right vibrations.

'Colette, stop,' I say. 'We don't need them.'

'We do, though.' She looks at me and her eyes fill with tears. 'People are going to die if we don't end this.'

'We'll end it,' I say. 'Without their help.'

Mr and Mrs Latchitt start laughing again, and I've never wanted to punch anyone in the face more.

'Trust me,' I say. 'Trust me.'

She bites her lip and nods. I turn to Gus. 'Do it,' I say.

Gus drops the worm on to Mrs Latchitt's face, and then throws the cup full of them at Mr

Latchitt as he lunges towards them. I grab Colette's hand at the same time that Hal and Naira let go of Mrs Latchitt, and the three of them lead us to the back of the maze and out of the exit while the Latchitts fight off the worms. I hear Mrs Latchitt shrieking as the ghost train door closes behind us, and we sprint back towards the fairground.

I guess it's all on me now.

CHAPTER TWENTY-EIGHT

A PARTICULAR KIND OF MAGIC

'Head for the control hut,' I shout, as we run through flying missiles, smoke and general chaos. 'I'll explain when we get there.'

'This is insane,' Gus says, as we pass the helter-skelter which is literally on fire. Smoke is pouring out of the top window where Mr Canton stood only about half an hour earlier, and orange flames are flicking like snake tongues up the sides of the building.

'Under here,' I say, pointing to the small space under the steps of the hut, which will give us at least a bit of shelter from the debris shooting around the green. We crawl into the dark hollow and try to catch our breath.

'Anyone have any idea how to work the control panel in there?' I point at the hut above us.

They all shake their heads.

'Why?' Naira asks.

'I think I know how to kill the brain-biters,' I say. 'Not just put them to sleep. Finish them.'

'What do you need?' Hallie says.

'We need to be able to work the control panel, and something that makes a properly low, growly noise. Loads of bass, like grime or drill music.'

'Except none of our phones are working, thanks to the Latchitts,' Colette says.

'Hold up.' Gus's face lights up and he starts to stand. 'I have an idea. Naira, I need your super-brain, and Hal, I need your rage-strength. Come help.'

'What about me?' Colette says.

'You need to stay hidden in case the Latchitts come looking. You and Angelo should wait here.'

Gus runs off across the green. 'Ha! Dodged it!' he whoops, as an unidentified metal object just misses his head. 'Come on!' he yells at Nai and Hal.

'Anyone know what he's thinking?' Hallie asks.

'No clue,' Naira sighs. 'But it had better be good.'

They run off after him and all three of them disappear into the smoke.

Colette and I crouch in the darkness under the hut. The smoke in the air is thickening, and toxic-smelling fumes fill the space around us. There's nothing clean to breathe. We cover our mouths and noses as well as we can, and for a moment I close my eyes. With the noise and chaos around us being muffled by the blanket of smoke, I can almost imagine that we're safe under here together.

'Peekaboo!' A masked face appears out of the smoke on one side of the hut at the same time as a massive pair of arms grab Colette from behind.

Colette screams and tries to dig her feet into the ground as she's dragged backwards. I still have her hand, and I grasp it harder as she starts slipping away from me.

'Angelo!' Colette shouts, and she's crying and fighting and trying to yank herself out of Mr Latchitt's grasp.

I reach for her other hand and manage to get my arms around her, locking my fingers together and clinging on with every bit of strength I have. I pull us down to the ground, knowing it will make it harder for the Latchitts to wrench us out. I kick out at Mr Latchitt with my good leg. Colette does the same to Mrs Latchitt.

There's a moment as Mr Latchitt jerks Colette backwards when I feel my grip on her slip. So I squeeze my fingers together harder behind her back and pull her closer.

'I'm not letting go,' I yell.

We struggle for a few moments, but I know

we have time on our side and they don't. They need to get away. We just have to hang on.

Then suddenly the pull on Colette stops. The hands withdraw. Mrs Latchitt's masked face disappears into the smoke again. But Colette and I don't let go of each other. We just sit under the hut, trying to catch our breath, bracing ourselves for another attack.

'What up, Gs?' Gus's face appears out of the gloom. 'Oh soz, am I interrupting something? My bad.' He sniggers in a way that makes me want to bring up cousin Julia again.

'The Latchitts tried to snatch Col,' I say, still reluctant to let her go, just in case. 'Have they gone?'

'No sign of them,' Gus says. 'And I brought backup.'

Over his shoulder I see Mo and Kai, holding a bunch of cables, and looking like they've just emerged from the trenches after a ten-year war. Behind them a huge, dark shape moves through the smoke. It's Shaheed, straining to pull a trailer the size of a Mini Cooper, with Hal and Naira pushing from behind.

Col and I carefully pull ourselves out from under the hut and help the others to wheel the trailer as close to the hut as possible. As I get behind it, I realise the trailer is carrying an industrial generator – the ones that power the big rides. It's a monster, and though it's switched off right now, I can imagine what the noise will be like when it's switched on. Gus is a genius.

'You swear we can claim the points, yeah?' Shaheed looks at Gus suspiciously.

'Would I do you wrong, bro?' Gus says. 'You get the points. We just want to witness the greatest mass flinch of all time, and we don't have the skillz.'

'Shift then,' Shaheed says, and runs up the steps to the control hut and pulls the broken door from what's left of its hinges, throwing it off the side of the steps.

The rest of us squish into a corner while Mo and Kai stand at the panel.

'Mo and Kai are the sound engineers for the Year 7 performance,' Gus says with a grin, as they turn on the power and expertly twist knobs and hook up wires, attaching an extension cord to the microphone and then feeding it out of the hut and down to the generator. Shaheed and Naira run back outside and fix the microphone to the trailer, and give us the thumbs up to say they're ready.

'Gus, you legend!' Colette says.

'More than just a pretty face,' he says. 'General assist, baby, it's the only way to live.'

'It needs to be on maximum volume,' I say. 'Like glass-shatteringly loud.'

'On it,' Mo grunts, sliding up some bars while Kai checks the connection to the microphone.

Shaheed is waiting by the power-on switch for the generator, looking up at us, his hand hovering over the controls. He is desperate to flick that switch.

'Do it, man,' Gus yells.

Shaheed flicks the switch on the generator

and it fires up with a roar, the intensity of the noise shaking the trailer. It's painfully loud where we're standing so close to it, but when the sound hits the mic and blasts out of the fairground speakers, it's like nothing I've ever heard before. It's almost unbearable.

The whole fairground seems to buzz and shudder. We instinctively put our hands over our ears, but it hardly makes a difference. The vibrations go through my teeth and bones until I feel like my entire body is going to explode. I hear the pop of speakers as they blow, unable to manage the insane number of decibels running through them. And then, when enough of the speakers have blown that the noise starts to die down, Shaheed flicks the switch.

The generator judders, and stops, and the whole world seems to go quiet and still.

'Did everyone flinch?' Shaheed yells, rubbing the back of his neck. The mic is still on, so his voice echoes around the fairground over the few remaining speakers that haven't blown out.

The air fills with the screech of feedback.

'I think you're good,' Gus yells back.

Mo and Kai fist-bump each other, turn off the power to the sound desk and we all pile down the steps of the hut and back out on to the grass.

'Thanks,' I say to Mo, Kai and Shaheed. 'You guys are the ultimate Flinch champions.'

'Sweet,' Shaheed says. 'Bored of Flinch now actually. Let's get milkshakes.' And he, Mo and Kai walk off into the smoky fair like the past two hours never even happened.

The rest of us look at each other.

'The bees?' Hallie asks.

'Stopped,' Colette says. 'I feel normal. Sort of.'

'Yeah,' I say. It's like all the tension in my body that's been building up over the last few weeks has been released. Like a deflating balloon. I'm bone tired, but in a good way. 'Let's check our necks.'

Colette turns and lifts her hair. I feel the back

of her neck and behind her ears. 'Nothing,' I say. 'It's either asleep or dead.'

'Same here.' Naira is poking at Gus again.

'I reckon it's dead,' Gus says. 'Because Naira poking with her witch fingers would wake anything up.'

Colette checks me, and Gus checks Naira. All clear.

'There's only one way to be properly sure, though,' Hallie says. 'And we can't do that on our own.'

'You mean we need doctors,' Naira says. 'Scans and tests, like they did for Michelle.'

'Let's go check on Mr Canton,' I say. Because I've been thinking the same thing.

We cover our mouths and noses and run across the war zone that was once Finches Green. Everything is trashed. At least three fires are burning. Dread Wood kids are sitting on the ground by the fairground speakers, rubbing their necks, looking totally done in and like they've just woken up from a bad dream.

'Hey, look.' I stop running and point at the ground. We all gather around the puddle of brain-biters, still lying in the spot where someone barfed them up. They're completely still, not even a twitch. Gus pokes at them with the toe of his shoe and they scatter, their bodies rigid.

'They look pretty dead to me,' he says. 'They're crispier than my grandma's hair.'

Hallie stomps on a couple and they practically disintegrate. 'Deffo dead, I'd say.'

'Thank god,' Colette says, stomping on some more like she's trying to crack a hole in the earth's crust. 'Just making sure.'

We don't have time to stomp on every brain-biter in Finches Green, no matter how much we want to, so we get moving again. I'm relieved to see Mr Canton exactly where we left him, semi-conscious and humming 'Pop Goes the Weasel'.

'I never want to hear that tune again for the rest of my life,' Colette says, as we run over to him.

'My crew!' Mr C's face lights up. 'Did you find my whistle?'

'Sorry, sir,' Hallie says. 'We got distracted. A lot has happened.'

'RIP whistle.' Mr C closes his eyes for a few seconds. Then he looks up at us, the goofy, dazed expression on his face clearing for a moment. 'Are you all OK?'

'We're fine,' Naira says. 'But we really need to talk to you.'

Mr C nods. 'Understood. You know my office door is always open. Even if I'm bleeding from the head.'

'Two of us should run for help,' I say. 'Find someone with a working phone and call an ambulance.'

But as I'm saying it, I hear the sound of sirens and see flashing blue lights pierce the clouds of smoke.

Gus runs to the end of the trailer and looks out at the fairground. 'It's the fire brigade, police and an ambulance,' he calls back. 'I'll get someone for Mr C.' He disappears into the smoke again.

'They're going to want answers,' Colette says. 'Where do we even start?'

'They didn't believe us last time,' Hallie says. 'I don't see how it's going to be any different now.'

'Maybe they didn't believe us,' I say. 'Or maybe they know exactly what's been going on and the Latchitts have got to them.'

'You leave them to me,' Mr Canton says, struggling to get to his feet. Naira and I go either side of him and prop him up. 'You know what they say . . . If anyone can . . .'

'. . . Canton can,' we say together.

'That's right, my slimes. They don't call me "The GOAT" for no reason.'

We let him off with the smallest of eye-rolls.

CHAPTER TWENTY-NINE

HOMECOMING

After a grim weekend spent clearing up Finches Green with the rest of the school, and days of lectures from Mr Hume about how badly we let Dread Wood High and ourselves down – unacceptable behaviour even if we were under the influence of a mystery parasite – it's a relief when things start to get back to normal.

On Wednesday evening, Naira and I turn on to Hallie's road to see Colette and Gus sitting on her garden wall looking bruised but happy. The weather has changed over the weekend, from spring clinging on to the dregs of winter, to spring turning its face to summer. The sky is blue, the air has lost its bite, and the perfect gardens on Hallie's street are filling with perfect flowers in perfect brightly coloured rows.

'Hey.' Colette jumps up. She has daisies in her hair and her freckles are already starting to come out, but under her hoodie I know she's covered in bruises.

I grin at her and she surprises me with a massive hug.

'Don't back away, Naira,' Colette says, hugging her too. 'Everyone gets cuddles from now on, whether they like it or not.'

'Oh god, I thought we'd left all the horror behind us,' Naira says, but she's smiling and she hugs back.

'Five full minutes she hugged me for,' Gus says. 'She nearly burst my stoma bag.'

'I'm just so glad to have you guys in my life,' Colette says. She looks like she might cry.

'Because we lead you into life-or-death, apocalypse-type situations?' Gus says. 'You're weird, Colette.'

'You know why,' she sniffs.

And we do. Because we wouldn't let her sacrifice herself, no matter how bad things were. Because we won't let anything come between us.

'Well, I am irresistible,' Gus says. 'Cousin Julia says so every New Year's when she's had a sip of champagne and eaten too much apple tart.'

We all crack up laughing.

'Here she comes,' Naira says, and we turn to watch Hal's mum's car pulling into her drive, Hallie waving from the passenger seat with the biggest smile on her face.

'Here,' Colette says, pulling some fabric out of her bag. 'Grab an end.'

We unravel the cloth and hold up the 'Welcome Home, Michelle!' banner that we made over the weekend. And when I say made, I mean Colette did most of the work, I coloured in some of the lettering, Gus painted a picture of a chicken that looks more like a cow, and Naira added the comma after 'Home'.

'You guys, this is awesome!' Hallie says, as her mum opens the boot of the car and carefully lifts out the animal carrier. 'We'll take her, Mum.'

Hallie carries the crate and we all follow her through to the garden and down the path to Michelle's enclosure. Colette and Naira tie the banner to the chicken wire so Michelle can see it, and Hallie, Gus and I settle Michelle back into her home.

After Hal's made a big fuss of Michelle, and she's majestically strutting around like she's never been infected with a brain-biting parasite, we step out of the enclosure and close the gate.

Colette gives Hallie a hug that almost knocks her off her feet.

'Apparently, we hug now,' Gus says to Hallie, who's looking at us like she doesn't know what the hell's happening. 'And not just on special occasions or if we're pumped up on ten millimetres of parentally approved alcohol and apple tart.'

'Right,' Hallie says, while the rest of us laugh.

Gus sniffs the air. 'I smell artisan crisps,' he whoops, and runs off towards the garden tables where Hallie's mum has put out snacks.

'What do you think will happen next?' Colette asks, when we're sitting and stuffing our faces.

I swallow a mouthful of Coke. 'I think we're as safe as we can be for now, thanks to Mr C backing us up with the police.'

'Although after what the Latchitts said, we don't know if we can *really* trust the police, or anyone in an adult position of responsibility,' Gus says.

'They can't all be dirty though, right?' Colette says.

'No.' Naira shakes her head. 'I don't think they can all be under the Latchitts' control. There are lots of people who can't be corrupted.'

'But we'll have to be even more careful from now on.' Hallie looks over her shoulder to make sure her mum's not listening. 'And not just with the cops. Anyone could be working with the Latchitts.'

'Who do you think they wanted you to meet, Col?' Gus says, opening a second bag of crisps.

Colette gets that hard look on her face again. 'Don't know, don't care. I want nothing to do with any part of their family.'

We all eat in silence for a moment. I wonder if Colette isn't at least a bit curious to know who the Latchitts were going to introduce her to. I know I am.

'The good news is that your worms are officially dead, though.' Hallie opens a pack of luxury biscuits.

'But not gone,' Gus says with a shudder.

'They will be soon,' I say. 'When the hospital scanned me they said that the carcass is already being absorbed into my body.'

Naira shudders. 'I hate the thought of that thing becoming a part of me.'

'We might develop brain-biter powers,' Colette says.

'Awesome,' Gus gasps. 'Imagine the possibilities.'

'We're not getting brain-biter powers,' Naira tuts. 'Look at Michelle – she had one and she's totally normal.'

Hallie grins. 'Parasite free and loving life.'

'Behold.' Gus waves his arm towards Michelle's enclosure. 'The chicken of hope. May we look to her when dark days return to remind us that all is not lost.'

'When dark days return,' Colette says. 'They will, won't they? The Latchitts aren't going to let us get away with ruining their experiment.'

'They'll be back,' Naira says. 'And lucky you, Colette, they probably *really* hate you too now.'

'Welcome to the gang,' Hallie says, shoving a whole biscuit in her mouth. 'You're now an official member of Club Loser. You'll love it here.' Bits of crumb and chocolate fly everywhere.

'But until they return to wreak a savage revenge on us, we go back to eating crisps and watching funny stuff on the internet,' says Gus.

'Truly the stuff that life was made for.'

Colette smiles, but I know she's worried. I don't blame her.

'Whatever happens,' I say. 'We stick together. I told you I wouldn't let you go, and I meant it. And that goes for all of you weirdos.'

'Same,' Colette answers.

'Totally,' Hallie says.

'You know I'm down for that.' Gus winks and salutes for some reason.

Naira nods. 'Yeah. Agreed.'

There are a few seconds of silence as we all look around at each other, then Gus breaks it with, 'Can I get an amen?'

We all groan and throw crisps at him. And then we put the Latchitts to the backs of our minds and eat, talk and laugh until the sun starts to set behind the trees of the Dread Wood.

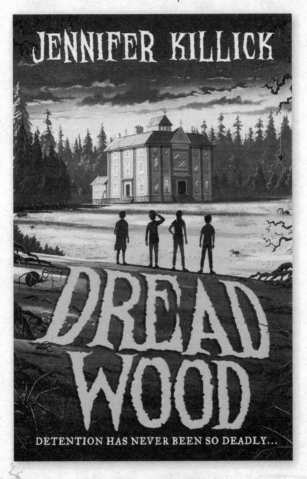

LOOK OUT FOR THE NEXT
THRILLING BOOK IN THE SERIES,
COMING SOON!

JENNIFER KILLICK

Jennifer Killick is the author of the *Dread Wood* series, *Crater Lake*, *Crater Lake, Evolution* and the *Alex Sparrow* series. Jennifer regularly visits schools and festivals, and her books have been selected four times for the Reading Agency's Summer Reading Challenge. She lives in Uxbridge, in a house full of children, animals and books. When she isn't busy mothering or step-mothering (which isn't often) she loves to watch scary movies and run as fast as she can, so she is fully prepared for witches, demons, and the zombie apocalypse.